"As small as a bird's pecking or sipping, things all are predestined and predestining." Buddhist Scripture

"When the true is false, the false is true; / Where is nothing, there is everything." Cao Xueqing, *Dream of Red Chamber*

Also by the Author

FICTION

Death of a Red Heroine

A Loyal Character Dancer

When Red Is Black

A Case of Two Cities

Red Mandarin Dress

The Mao Case

Don't Cry, Tai Lake

Enigma of China

Shanghai Redemption

Becoming Inspector Chen

POETRY

Lines around China

Poems of Inspector Chen

SHORT STORY

Years of Red Dust

Inspector Chen and Me

Qiu Xiaolong

Inspector Chen and Me

Copyright © 2018 by Qiu Xiaolong.

All rights reserved. No part of this book shall be reproduced, stored in a retrieval system, or transmitted, in any form or by any means without the prior written permission of the author.

First published in the United States of America in Sept 2018

ISBN: 9781720197720

To my friend Norman Ding

Contents

Confidence First-Gained

Because of Doctor Zhivago (I, II)

Overseas Chinese Lu

Inspector Chen with Louis Vuitton in Longhua Temple

What Might Have Happened to Chen Cao (I, II, III)

Confidence First Gained

In the early days of the Cultural Revolution, one of the commonly seen scenes in China was that of "revolutionary mass criticism" staged against "class enemies."

There was no official definition for the nationwide movement. To begin with, it had little to do with "criticism" in the proper sense of the word. It came close, if anything, to public denunciation and humiliation of the target in question. Among the generally accepted rationales for the "revolutionary mass criticism," one of them was to rally the proletariat and to demoralize the "class enemies," which could also bring in a lot of defining and redefining. In accordance to Mao's class struggle theory, the struggle between socialism and capitalism exists throughout the long, long socialist period till the final realization of communism. For the proletariat, the class enemies consequently comprise landlords, rich farmers, counter revolutionaries, bad elements, and rightist in the late 1950s, and then for an expanded category during the Cultural Revolution, capitalists, unreformed intellectuals, historical counter-revolutionaries, and capitalist-roaders, the last being a newly-coined term in reference to "the Party officials pushing along the capitalist road against Chairman Mao." For the long and the short of it, those were class enemies to the revolution people, consequently, the unmistakable target of the proletarian dictatorship.

As a rule, the format of revolutionary mass criticism involved the class enemies being marched onto a temporary stage or a cordoned area under a large portrait of Mao, with their heads hung low in repentance, weighed down by the name-bearing blackboards hung around their necks, and for a popular variation, further demonized with tall white paper hats symbolic of devils of the netherworld. Organizations like Red Guards (in schools) or Worker Rebels (in factories, but sometimes referred to as Red Guards as well) made indignant denouncements on the stage, with the revolutionary mass audience shouting slogans in thunderous response and raising their fists high in the air.

For a real example, Liu Shaoqi, the Chairman of the People's Republic of China, then seen as the arch rival to Mao Zedong, the Chairman of the Chinese Communist Party, had to face such a revolutionary mass criticism, and that with his wife Wang Guangmei groveling aside, wearing a badly-torn, bosom-and-thigh revealing mandarin dress and a fake necklace made of ping pang balls—the dress and necklace both being emblematic of bourgeois decadency. Liu Shaoqi died, and like him, most of the class enemies suffered savage beating at the heat of the revolutionary mass criticism, and quite a number of them beaten to death.

Before 1949, Father ran a small perfume factory, hence a "capitalist" in Mao's class system, though with his factory gone in the movement of "transferring private-owned enterprises to the state-owned" in the mid-1950s. At the beginning of Cultural Revolution, he had to go through revolutionary mass criticism at the state-owned factory. Initially, I knew little about his ordeal. But back home one evening, he lurched toward me with a sudden limp and fell, and another evening, his face showed undisguisable large bruises like a rotten persimmon. With all of us gone to bed, he still had to work and rework on something called "guilty plea" late into the night, three or four evenings a week.

The ritual of guilty-plea-writing was hailed as a new development against the class enemies, who had to repent their sins and crimes, and in his case, with a focus on his exploitation of the workers before 1949. That should not have been too difficult, I imagined, with the contents being so familiar to him. Basically, he paid himself much more than the four or five workers under him, and pocketed most of the profit or "surplus value," a term I had just learned in school, and that's all about it. But the Red Guards, instead of letting him off the hook easily, made a point of demanding him to denounce the "atrocious crimes" from the bottom of his black capitalist heart, again and again, until to their sadistic satisfaction.

In the third year of the Cultural Revolution, Father broke down with acute retina detachment, so the "revolutionary committee" of the factory told him not to come to work anymore. He left there not without a touch of relief. At least no more revolutionary mass criticism for him.

But that gave rise to another problem. In the light of the proletarian dictatorship, the sick leave benefit was possible only for the proletariat, but not for a capitalist like him. In other words, no pay, nor medical insurance for him. Because of his class status, Mother's pay got drastically reduced too, far from enough to support the family. Half way back home, he came to the realization that he had to have the eye surgery done as soon as possible—and then to go back to work.

So he managed to check into the Shanghai ENT Hospital the next day. Hopefully just one or two days for the surgery, and then a week or so for recovery. In the meantime, he would not have to worry about revolutionary mass criticism—at least not for that short period.

But things at the hospital turned out to be totally different those days. With a large number of experienced doctors and nurses condemned as "black monsters," the remaining ones were too busy struggling for survival. Consequently, the patients there had to go through an unexpectedly longer waiting period for operation due to the severe staff shortage.

On the third day, a message came home through the neighborhood phone service: "The family member of the Bed Seventeen hurry over to the hospital for revolutionary mass criticism."

"Bed Seventeen" referred to Father, his bed being so numbered in the hospital ward. The message was from a Red Guard organization called "Expelling Tigers and Leopards," with its name derived from a Mao poem. That threw our whole family into panic.

How could he have gotten into trouble at the hospital? And for that matter, why should the family member also go there and report to the Red Guards?

Mother had recently suffered a nervous breakdown. My elder brother Xiaowei was practically paralyzed, and my younger sister Xiaohong was too young to help. So the job was up to me. The realization hit home with a splitting headache. Having heard stories about the family members being mass-criticized together with the "black monsters," I shuddered at the prospect. A "black puppy," I had long given up any dream of becoming a Red Guard, going to college, or getting a decent job, but those would be the worries for the future, nothing like the revolutionary mass criticism for the day.

Mother served me a bowl of mint-flavored green bean soup, my favorite in summer, but it helped little with my terrible headache. I rose to leave for the hospital with reluctance bordering on resentment.

Along the way, I tried to figure out the possible cause of his trouble. The Red Guards at the factory being unaware of his surgery, they could not have reported his black class status to the Red Guards at the hospital. He should have known better to reveal it to others. I literally cudgeled my brains out, yet without a clue, sweating and steaming in a bus tight-packed like a bamboo steamer of tiny soup buns. At the hospital stop, I stumbled down, drained like one of the broken buns.

Instead of heading to the ward, I paid a visit first to the office of the ENT Hospital Revolutionary Committee.

As it turned out, Expelling Tigers and Leopards was an organization consisted of the patients rather than the hospital staff members, who were hardly capable of protecting themselves, drowning like "the clay images drifting across the river" in a Chinese proverb. The revolutionary organization came into existence overnight, in response to Mao's urgent call that the proletarian dictatorship has to be enforced into every corner of the society.

The head of the Red Guard organization, who gave orders in the ward next to Father's, was a patient surnamed Huang—Commander Huang, wearing a red armband on his T-shirt sleeve, and white gauze pad around his throat. It was said that Commander Huang suffered from esophageal cancer at an advanced stage,

"It's our Party's policy to be humanistic even toward the sick class enemies, but not for an unremorseful one," Commander Huang began, his voice hissing with a sudden metal sharpness. "Not until he truly repents his crimes to the full, he deserves no medical treatment whatsoever here. Don't dream the big dream that he could get away so easily."

"You're absolutely right, Commander Huang," I said in a hurry. Under the normal circumstances, it might not be a too big deal for Father to write and rewrite the "guilty plea" for a couple of times more, but the lacking of Commander Huang's approval here spelled that no doctor would be allowed to perform the surgery on him, and as a result, Father had to stay here for weeks, or even months. As it was, we had a hard time making the ends meet at home, not to mention all the hospital expense.

I kept nodding like a wound-up robot, but I was not a real robot, rankling with the insufferable humiliation of such a role for me to play.

"Instead of repenting the bourgeois life style of his," Commander Huang continued huskily, as if whistling through a broken steel pipe, "he brags and boasts about it even at the hospital. He has to write a new guilty plea."

"Yes, I will help him write a soul-searching statement," I said mechanically, recollecting the words and sentences I had heard at the revolutionary mass criticism at school. "Please give me some specific details, Commander Huang, so I can make him dig deeper into his black heart and soul and come to terms with the very root of the evil."

"Well, he talks as if he alone knew how to make a cup of milk powder drink," Commander Huang said, "thanks to his extravagant life style in the old society. Who the devil is he to look down on the working class people?"

Siren started piercing through the back of my mind. At home, Father had told us very little about himself before 1949—for fear of "advocating the bourgeois life style." More often than not, he wrapped himself in a cocoon of stubborn silence. There was perhaps only one exception. During the so-called three years of natural disasters at the beginning of sixties, with over thirty million Chinese people dying of starvation under Mao's campaign of Three Red Flags, Father too was staved into delirious reminiscence of a special Russian restaurant meal plan he had enjoyed in the mid-1940s. In accordance to the plan, he could have as much milk as he liked, seven days of a week. Not necessarily fresh milk all the time, he caught glimpses of a blond waitress making milk powder drink expertly behind the counter. But that sounded even more exotic to me, really like as a mouth-watering fairy tale. At the time, I did not have a bottle of milk for the whole year.

Now by the side of Bed Seventeen, I did not have the heart, however, to complain at the sight of a much-changed Father, unshaven, unkempt, blindfolded with some liquid dropped in prior to the surgery. Fumbling, he failed even to take my hand, let alone a pen. So that's the reason Commander Huang wanted me to the hospital to help, I realized, noticing a jar of milk powder on the bedside table for the next bed patient.

I drew in a deep breath, trying to gather from him the details of the trouble-causing incident. In the middle of the Cultural Revolution, milk powder became more of a rarity. Bed Eighteen was lucky enough to get a jar of it, but he did not know how to properly mix it, resulting in an inedible mess. Father told him the knack of stirring with a little cold water first before pouring in hot water, and he mentioned his meal plan in the Russian restaurant by way of explanation. Sure enough, it made all the difference. Bed Eighteen then talked to others about it with such great gusto, it soon spread out of the ward. The same evening, Commander Huang made inquiries into it, and detected the problem with his ever-present alertness for anything new in the class struggle.

But the pressing issue for me was how to rewrite the plea, which had to be an acceptable one—in the new light of a cup of milk powder. It would not do by just piling up apologies, however truthfully contrite, for his bourgeois decadent life style. I reexamined Father's rejected piece, which began, too bookishly, from the beginning.

It started with how as a high school student, he had dreamed of a college education, but upon graduation, he was compelled to find a job to help the family, working as an accountant for a Dutch trade company. When the company folded up without any warning in the late 1940s, he was offered, in lieu of a severance pay, an unsold case of perfume essence. Unable to land another job, he turned to the essence as the last resort, struggling with an English booklet on perfume manufacturing. Experimenting by adding water and alcohol and whatever liquid imaginable, and mixing them with all the makeshift equipment available in the shikumen courtyard, he succeeded producing a tiny bottle of cologne, on which Mother put on a label "flower-dew-water," smiling, sweating beside the moss-covered sink. A company started up just like that, pushing out a new popular brand of perfume among the upper-middle class Shanghai wives.

Now that part of his pre-1949 experience he had never shared with us before, which I learned for the first time in the hospital ward that afternoon. The pen trembling in my hand, I came to see the problem for the guilty plea—in the eyes of Commander Huang—in which Father appeared to be a victim through the circumstances, an accidental capitalist, so to speak.

The blindfolded "capitalist" started dictating for the new piece, but I decided not to follow him closely. The way he was trying, the guilty pleas was bound to be rejected again. In the school, in a big-character guilty plea posted on the wall, one of my "black monster teachers" condemned himself so voluminously, I recalled, like a Sichuan chef ever so generously throwing in handfuls and handfuls of peppers. *"I am totally rotten, black from heart to toe... For my crime, I should be trodden underfoot, unable to turn over for hundreds of years... For fattening myself on the poor people, I deserve to be cut for thousands of cuts..."*

Like in a proverb, a dead pig does not have to worry about the scaling water, which cannot make it any more dead. Why not piling up those revolutionary clichés in Father's statement?

I included that milk powder part, of course, as an early but unmistakable sign of his decadent indulgence. So his eventual turning into a capitalist was anything but accidental.

About forty five minutes late, I plodded into the conclusion, jotting down an exclamation mark, nodding to myself, when I heard an announcement coming through a loud speaker in the hospital ward,

"Bed Seventeen and his family member come out to the hospital reception hall."

There, the first thing I saw was a long red banner stretched across the half-deserted hall: **The Hospital Revolutionary Mass Criticism**.

Apparently, Commander Huang seized upon my availability to have the event arranged in addition to the guilty plea writing, for Father, blindfolded, was unable to go through the ritual without somebody else taking him by hand. I turned over the guilty plea to Commander Huang, who stuffed it into his pant pocket without taking a look, and gestured me to take my position standing beside Father, whose neck was presently weighed down with a heavy blackboard showing his name written and crossed out in color chalk. There were two other patients standing aligned with him, each of them sporting a blackboard round his and her neck.

"Lower your heads and plead guilty to our great leader Chairman Mao!" Commander Huang hissed out the command.

Standing aside, I found my head hung lower in spite of myself, though without a blackboard around my neck—the only difference between father and son. The humiliation overwhelming, Father soon proved too weak to stand still, putting a hand on my shoulder for support.

I tried imagining myself into a human crutch, stiff, sturdy, unbreakable, without thinking or feeling. The effort was not that successful, though.

It was perhaps because of his throat problem that Commander Huang did not say anything else there. He stepped off to return with a chair and sat there through the ritual.

At the end of the longest hour in my memory, Commander Huang cleared his throat and waved us away.

I decided to stay on by Father's side, believing there would be more rewriting for me to do there. No point going home and then hurrying back to the hospital. I felt drained.

But by the time I finally decided to leave the hospital around nine thirty that evening, I still heard nothing from Commander Huang.

No message the next morning, either. Around the noon, I double-checked with the neighborhood phone service. Still no phone message from Expelling Tigers and Leopards at the hospital. Inexplicable. Our whole family was like ants crawling on a hot wok. On the third day, a phone message finally came: Father was being sent into the operation room, and he would be released for home the next day.

So Commander Huang must have given approval to the guilty plea; failing that, the doctors would not have moved ahead with the surgery

It was to my credit then—the new guilty plea got approved with all the creative words and phrases I had thrown in like Sichuan pepper without Father's knowledge.

But there were some other possible scenarios, I thought. Commander Huang might have relented at the sight of a kid trembling like a broken reef during the revolutionary mass criticism; alternatively, he could have suffered an unexpected turn for the worse in his own condition. Whatever interpretations, with the Cultural Revolution engulfing the whole country, it was but the storm in a cup of milk powder drink, after all.

"You have done the mission impossible," Mother said, subscribing to the scenario that held out the laurel to me.

It's the first time that I gained any confidence for myself, of all things, in writing a guilty plea.

Because of Doctor Zhivago

I

It was a summer night in the year of 1962 when a group of special police came out of the blue, rushing into Red Dust Lane, making a raid on Mr. Ma's Bookstore next to the side entrance of the lane. Two or three hours later, they snatched Mr. Ma away in handcuffs, with Mrs. Ma running barefoot behind them, weeping, begging, all the way out on Fujian Road.

It threw the whole lane in confusion.

"Mr. Ma can hardly harm a fly," Dehua, one of the neighbors of the Mas in the same *shikumen* building, whispered in puzzlement. "Why?"

It turned into a question shared by many in the lane, but little could they do about it. It was a matter of course for cops to whisk someone away without making an explanation or showing a warrant. That was what the proletarian dictatorship was all about. The Party authorities decided everything—and every case too. No attorney, no jury, and no court. No question about it either.

"We have to believe in the Party authorities. There must be a reason for it. Our government will never wrong an innocent man. If Mr. Ma is to be found not guilty, he will soon be released," Comrade Jun, the head of the neighborhood committee, said earnestly in a lane meeting.

Such a speech was of course politically correct, but it did not throw any light on the mystery. For a police raid like that, the less said, the better, that much people knew. So all they did was to try to console the inconsolable Mrs. Ma, who remained in tears all day, repeating over and over that she knew nothing about the cause of her husband's trouble.

When the news came that Mr. Ma could be sentenced as a counter-revolutionary, the lane was immediately shut up like shivering cicadas in the approaching winter.

Except for a young man, or to be more exact, a boy of thirteen or fourteen, who was not a resident of the lane, but regular customer to the bookstore, named or surnamed Cao. As Mrs. Ma later recalled, Cao must have read all the Chinese translations of Sherlock Holmes available in the store without buying a single copy. So he was perhaps eager to try his hand like a "private investigator," gathering information about Mr. Ma, particularly at the "evening talk" in front of the lane.

Such an "unofficial investigation" appealed to the collective curiosity of the lane. A file was soon formed about Mr. Ma.

According to it, Mr. Ma had grown up in the lane. In 1948, just one year before the Communists took over the power, he inherited from his father a small bookstore consisting of a front room opening onto Fujian Road, and a back room leading into the lane. With the new class system that came into effect in the early fifties, he was classified as a "small business owner," merely one shade less black than a "capitalist" in the new socialist China. It was such a tiny bookstore, however, where he worked by himself, incapable of exploiting anyone—not even in the light of the Marxist surplus value theory.

He renamed the bookstore as "Mr. Ma's," in a subtle allusion to a poor, idiosyncratic scholar in *Stories of Scholars*, a classical Ming dynasty novel. An equally poor, idiosyncratic bookseller, Mr. Ma kept extra-long business hours, sometimes as late as eleven or twelve at night. He was fond of quoting a proverb, "It always benefits you to read books." So he made a point of not driving away those penniless customers standing and reading there for hours, a small group that included Cao.

Mr. Ma was amiable to his neighbors, despite the fact he did not mix too much with them. To their questions about why he did not try to find a state-run company job, he would quote another old saying, "There's a beauty walking out of books, and there's a gold chamber appearing in books."

For Mr. Ma, at least the first part of the maxim proved to be true, as a beauty came to him, literally, out of books.

One late May evening, a young girl fainted in the store, still clutching a book in her hand. As it turned out, she had stood there for hours reading a poetry collection unaffordable to her, skipping her dinner. She had recently dropped out of college because of her poor health. He made her a bowl of hot beef noodles on a gasoline stove in the backroom, and gave her the copy of the poetry collection for free.

Several months later, to the surprise of the lane, he married her in the same backroom— now a wedding room for the two—with space just enough for a double bed, yet with a row of golden-ridged books shining above their headboard.

As the one and only decoration for the occasion, Mr. Ma chose to have a long silk scroll of calligraphy hung on the white wall: "To survive in a dry rut, two carps try to moisten each other with their saliva." It was a quote from Zhuangzi, an ancient Chinese philosopher about two thousand years earlier.

The bookstore then developed into a sort of husband-and-wife business. The two eccentric yet contented bookworms enjoyed every minute of their working together, wrapping themselves up in a cocoon of bookish imagination. Their neighbors regarded the two with a touch of tolerance, and of superiority too. After all, their "small private business" was nothing compared with the state-run enterprise that boasted of all the benefits of the new socialist system.

Because of their passion, the small bookstore with a well-chosen selection of books began spreading its name out of the neighborhood. Some college professors and newspaper reporters were said to be among the regular customers, including a well-known writer, who brought in a white-bearded foreigner with him. Mr. Ma knew a bit English and stored a small number of foreign language books as well. Mrs. Ma was a gracious host, serving a pot of Dragon Well tea for the special customers. The business appeared to be steadily picking up, which added to the visibility of the lane too.

Like in a Chinese proverb, however, there is no forecasting the change in the weather—and in the political weather too, for that matter.

Then came the special police force pounding on the door of Mr. Ma's bookstore that summer night.

There was something inexplicable about Mr. Ma's case, the neighbors agreed, so the possible clues from them assembled and analyzed in the "evening talk" helped little.

While confounded like others, Cao was still so young, like a young calf not yet afraid of the tiger. He went on with his investigation, collecting bits and pieces from the people in the lane. It was not an easy job. For a "current counter-revolutionary" case, Cao could not afford to appear to be too nosy, or he himself could have gotten into trouble. So he adopted an "approach of exclusion."

One possible cause for Mr. Ma's catastrophe, Chen speculated, could have been that of business tax evasion. The government authorities had been increasingly hard on the private business sector. During the "Three-Anti" campaign, a considerable number of business owners had been targeted and punished. But this neighborhood bookstore made little profit. Not much tax to talk about. And several neighbors were positive that Mr. Ma had never been audited.

Another possibility, though quite remote, would have been that of Mr. Ma's "bourgeois life style." A happy couple in all appearance, the Mas did not have a child—because of her health problem. Now according to Confucius, one of the most unfilial things imaginable under the sun would be for a man to go without offspring, and for Mr. Ma, a bookworm immersed in Confucian classics, that could have been a matter of crucial significance. Among the regular customers, there were also several young pretty college girls. But the neighbors all testified that the Mas were the best couple they had ever seen. Besides, it would have been out of the question for him to carry on behind her back; they stayed together practically all the time, in the store in front, or in the tiny room at the back.

Partially because of Cao's unwavering effort, people in the lane approached Comrade Jun, who refused to give out any information, except reiterating that Ma had been arrested as a current counter-revolutionary with the bookstore serving as "a secret black center of anti-socialism activity."

But "anti-socialism activity" sounded too much like a tall tale to the lane. Because of the location of the bookstore, whatever Mr. Ma might have been doing there could have been easily seen by the neighbors through the open door at the front, and through the half-open door at the back too. So they pressed Comrade Jun for explanation, who felt obliged to deliver another speech at a neighborhood meeting.

"According to Chairman Mao, the principal contradiction in our society is between the proletariat and capitalist, and throughout China's socialist period the danger of capitalist restoration continues to exist, so awareness of class struggle should be stressed day by day, month by month, and year by year. Now wat could those bourgeois intellectuals have been doing in the bookstore—staying there for hours, talking and discussing? Think about it, comrades. There are a lot of books anti-Party, and anti-socialism too."

But Cao remained unconvinced. It was nothing uncommon for people to stand browsing in the bookstore for hours, as he himself had done. Some of the lane residents also detected something suspicious about Comrade Jun, who looked troubled in his effort to answer others' questions. What's more, he seemed to be surreptitiously nice to Mrs. Ma, who was not without a graceful charm in her early thirties.

As a "family member of a counter-revolutionary," she had nowhere to turn for help. One of the feasible remedies, as suggested by her neighbors, would be to divorce Mr. Ma, so she could start from scratch, securing a new class status, if nothing else, for herself. These years, it was fairly common for a woman like her to denounce and divorce her husband in political trouble.

Considering Comrade Jun's Party cadre position, it did not appear that likely for him to make such a move to her. Still, there is no knowing for sure one's motive, as in those Sherlock Holmes stories.

But she swore to wait for the return of her husband despite the pressure. The front room—the bookstore—had been taken over by the neighborhood committee as a storage room for its propaganda material.

Refusing to send the remaining books to the recycle center, she moved all of them into the backroom, with hardly any space left for her to move around there. Sleepless at night, she would sometimes play a simple tune from a tiny music box, her neighbors heard. Not a revolutionary song, but the music box was said to be a gift from Mr. Ma, in addition to all the books.

"I'll keep the books until his return," she declared. "I can feel him in them."

But she could not live on them. Nor could she find a job with such a counter-revolutionary husband shadowing her around. So it was Comrade Jun who came up with a position proposal for her. To sweep the lane for the minimum pay—no more than seventy cents a day.

"It's necessary to carry out the proletarian dictatorship against the class enemy," he said, "but it did not mean that their family should starve to death."

The job, though not a desirable one, could be seen as practically created for her. Neither too heavy, nor requiring any particular skill. At the evening talk of the lane, people could not help suspecting an ulterior motive behind the surprisingly "humane" arrangement.

At their urging, Old Root, a respected figure in the lane, who had also read without buying in the erstwhile bookstore, agreed to take a look into it.

He dragged Comrade Jun out to a dumpling eatery on Zhejiang Road. There, after bowls of minced shrimp dumplings, a dish of sliced pig ears, and two bottles of nicely warmed sticky rice wine, Comrade Jun divulged that the trouble for Mr. Ma had come out of a foreign language book about a doctor surnamed Qi—Qi Wage, not that likely a Chinese name, but then those intellectuals could have made up strange names. Neither of them had ever heard of the book before, or of the doctor, either. Anyway, it was said to have been ordered by the higher authorities to put Mr. Ma into jail—a decision in the light of Chairman Mao's class struggle theory.

"But who would have reported the existence of such a book to the government authorities?" Old Root said, adding a large pinch of black pepper to the remaining dumpling soup. "No, I don't want to cause trouble for anybody. You don't have to worry about that, Comrade Jun. It's just that I have read so many books for free there. He's a nice man. And Mrs. Ma is such a pitiable woman."

"I understand," Comrade Jun said. "That's why I've tried to help. And there's something I don't really understand—something that might have caused Mr. Ma..."

As it turned out, Comrade Jun was concerned about her for a different reason. About two months earlier, Commissar Wen, a leading cadre in the district government, had held a meeting with a group of neighborhood cadres, focusing on the latest trend in the class struggle Mao had emphasized concerning the bourgeois intellectuals. Like in the past, the latest movement had to meet with a certain quota of class enemies for punishment. After the meeting, Commissar Wen questioned Comrade Jun about his silence during the discussion, and the latter came up with an excuse,

"Our lane is made mostly of ordinary people. No intellectuals, barely interested in anything out of the lane."

It was a true statement, but not what Commissar Wen would have liked to hear, who sat frowning with his back a stiff as a bamboo pole.

"Not all the people in your lane could be that simple and innocent, Comrade Jun. Red Dust Lane is known for something called the evening talk, I've heard a lot about it."

"Oh, the evening talk is just for fun," Comrade Jun said nervously. "In the summer, it's too hot for people to stay inside, so they sit outside talking before going to bed. As for any intellectuals in the lane, well, there's only one I can think of. Mr. Ma, who runs a small bookstore. But not exactly an intellectual. Self-educated. Not even with a college education. Nothing but a bookseller, and a bookworm too. He keeps saying that it always benefits you to read books."

"It always benefits you to read books" was an old proverb. Comrade Jun did not see anything wrong in it.

But he was wrong.

"What books?" Commissar Wen demanded even more sternly.

"There are so many books in the bookstore, you know."

"Yes, there are books and books, Comrade Jun. Class struggle is everywhere, even in a bookstore." Commissar Wen added after an emphatic pause. "As Chairman Mao has recently said, '**It's a new invention to write a novel in conspiracy against the Party**.'"

What Comrade Jun said in his response, he could have hardly remembered. He was too scared. Afterward, he kept wondering whether his panic-stricken response could have anything to do with the subsequent development at the bookstore, though he clung to the belief that he had not said anything incriminating Mr. Ma. Still, the head of the neighborhood committee remained secretly bothered. That accounted for his offer of help to Mrs. Ma.

Comrade Jun kept shaking his head at the end of the dumpling meal. Old Root ordered another bottle of rice wine and poured out a small cup for Comrade Jun.

"As long as you have not done anything wrong, Comrade Jun, you don't have to worry about a devil knocking at your door at night."

"I've made inquiries about Mao's latest instruction, but it's about a Chinese novel. Now for Mr. Ma, it's a foreign language book. That really beats me."

At the end of the summer, the mystery remained unsolved for the lane. Far, far away in Beijing, Mao repeated his warning about the danger of capitalist restoration through literature and art. As the head of the neighborhood committee, Comrade Jun declared again that it would be in everybody's interest in the lane not to talk any more about Mr. Ma. The political weather had been changing. No one could be too careful.

Old Root concurred in the evening talk of the lane, unfolding for some dramatic effect a white paper folding fan, which bore a line written by Zheng Banqiao, a Qing dynasty scholar. *It's not easy to be ignorant.*

"The line is so brilliant. Indeed, an old maxim put it so well: once a man starts reading and writing, he gets totally confused."

"But people have to know," Cao said, not yet ready to give up.

"For so many things in the world, you may never find the final explanation. Why bother that much?"

Cao's continuous effort was not without any result. He learned one more anecdote about Mr. Ma.

Mr. Ma made just one request in prison: to have some books brought in from the closed bookstore. Another surprise considering the cause of his trouble. The warden granted it on the condition that Mr. Ma could have only one book, and not a literary one.

Cao also succeeded in learning from a schoolmate, whose father was a senior officer in the city police bureau. According to the cop, the book in question had been banned in the Soviet Union. A Russian book about a Russian doctor. *Doctor Zhivago*. Being a foreign language book, it must have somehow escaped the police radar at first. Cao wondered how such a book, not yet translated into Chinese, could have harmed the socialist China, but he knew better to talk to the people in the evening talk of Red Dust Lane.

Old Root had tipped him that some people began to pay special attention to him—not a resident of the lane, but such a regular to the evening talk there.

One late December morning, during his last visit to the lane, Cao happened to see Mrs. Ma sweeping through the lane with a rough bamboo-slice broom, which loomed taller than her. It was cold. He shivered. And he thought of those days of his standing and reading in the bookstore for free, taking a cup of hot tea from her. He tried to say something, but without success.

The next moment, she vanished out of sight.

Nothing but a fallen yellow leaf stuck to a wet corner of the lane.

In a Tang dynasty poem, a fallen leaf awash in a rain pool served as a metaphor for a woman's forsaken loneliness, but he failed to recall whether he had read the poem in Mr. Ma's bookstore.

II

Mr. Ma was released in 1982, several years ahead of the time.

It came as a huge surprise to Red Dust Lane.

Even more so to Comrade Jun. Usually, the higher authorities would have contacted the neighborhood cadre first about such an unexpected development.

Things were changing, of course, after the Cultural Revolution. A number of "wrong cases" had been rectified. For instance, Chairman Liu Shaoqi, the Chairman of the People's Republic of China, had been wrongly accused by Chairman Mao Zedong, the Chairman of the Communist Party of China, and brutally killed like a naked rat in prison. Liu's pictures now reappeared in rehabilitation in the *People's Daily*, though Mao's portrait still hung high on Tiananmen Square.

Mr. Ma was nobody in comparison. Still, we were truly happy for Mrs. Ma in Red Dust Lane. Like in a Beijing opera about Wang Baochai, a virtuous wife in the seventh century, who waited for eighteen long years in an impoverished earthen cave for her husband, Mrs. Ma, too, finally had her man back, even though Mr. Ma was by no means like a triumphant general returning home in the Tang dynasty.

All these years, Mrs. Ma had fared worse than the heroine in the classical Beijing opera, sweeping the fallen leaves, day after day, in rain or shine. She turned into a taken-for-granted scene of the lane—a fragile woman dragging a long bamboo stick broom taller than herself, invariably carrying a humble smile on her face, and a plastic waste basket on her back. Surprisingly, her health appeared to have improved because of the physical labor. At least red spots were seen in her cheeks, though some people argued it was because of her constant exposure in the open. During the Cultural Revolution, she suffered humiliations and persecutions as a black family member, but probably not much worse than other "birds of the same black feathers." And she kept making her monthly visit to the prison. Eventually, the lane came to sort of respect her for the unwavering dedication to her husband.

"The man may not be too bad—no, not with a good wife remaining so loyal to him," Old Root commented at the news of Mr. Ma's release.

So a group of the lane residents poured out to the entrance of the lane that morning, waiting for him. For a wronged man, but also for a virtuous woman who believed in the innocence of her man.

It was then a totally changed Mr. Ma they witnessed—silver-haired and silver-browed like a white owl in the mountains. He dragged his unsteady steps into Red Dust Lane, leaning heavily on the shoulder of his frail wife, wearing a pair of glasses as thick as the bottoms of beer bottles, his eyes incessantly blinking in the sunlight. He was said to have damaged his vision reading too much in the dark prison cell. Nevertheless, the couple presented a touching sight of a white-haired man in the company of a rosy-cheeked woman, as if walking out of an old Chinese love story, though their age difference was not that large in reality.

Afterward, in a special neighborhood meeting, Comrade Jun delivered a well-prepared speech. "It was really politically necessary—in the early sixties—for the Party authorities to keep high alert against any possible sabotage attempt by the class enemies. All in the interests of the socialist China, as we understand. You, too, have to take a positive attitude toward the history, Mr. Ma. It is now correct, politically correct, of course, to redress those wrong cases. Look forward. Not backward. That is our Party's new slogan. If there's anything the neighborhood committee can do for you, please let us know."

"There's one thing the committee can do," Mr. Ma said slowly. "My wife does not mind going on with the lane-sweeping job, but I, too, have to do something."

That was a legitimate request. At his age, it was impossible for Mr. Ma to find a new job for himself. If he had worked at a state-owned company before, he might be able to go back to the same company. But he had not. No one claimed responsibility for that.

Comrade Jun suggested that the Mas resume their book business. It was providential that Mrs. Ma had kept those books, dust-covered, yet otherwise intact, in the backroom. In the mid-eighties, private bookstores or book booths started to reappear in the city. It should not be too difficult for them to have their license renewed, for which Comrade Jun offered to apply on their behalf. In addition, he returned to the old couple the front room which had been used for the storage of the neighborhood propaganda material. It was another surprise move to the lane, but no one really said anything. After all, the Mas had suffered so much for nothing.

"No, a bookstore will serve only as a daily reminder of my prison years," Mr. Ma said, blinking his eyes like an owl. Instead, he wanted to open a Chinese herbal medicine store in its place.

The next week, he submitted the license application. Comrade Jun took it upon himself to smooth the application process. Old Root too asked the audience at the evening talk to help in whatever way they could. Weeks passed with the application traveling from one bureaucratic desk to another, without making any progress. Mr. Ma looked more and more like a withered white owl, sighing in a hollow voice, which sounded like eerie hooting in the woods.

Then, of a sudden, a business license was express-delivered to Mr. Ma. As it turned out, somebody in the police bureau had put in a word for the old man. It confounded the lane. People had never heard of anything about Mr. Ma's connections there.

Whatever interpretation, a new signboard was made with the eye-catching name: Old Ma's Herbal Medicine Store.

"Congratulations, Mr. Ma! The Wheel of Fortune is finally turning in your favor." Comrade Jun added in an official tone, "The Party authorities are now encouraging private business in our socialist country."

"Thank you, Comrade Jun. We owe everything to the Party's new policy," Mrs. Ma said, clasping her fingers in a gesture of appreciation.

Amidst the people gathering in front of the herbal medicine store on its opening, Old Root struck a match to a long chain of firecrackers dangling from the tip of a bamboo pole in celebration. A practice that was no longer encouraged in the city for safety concerns, but for once it was acquiesced in the lane—because of its supposedly potency in scaring away the evil spirits associated with a place and ushering in the Fortune.

"You surely know your way around, Mr. Ma!" Old Root said in the chorus of the firecrackers. "Your business will surely gallop for thousands of mikes like a horse after a break!"

The comments referred to a combination of Mr. Ma's surname and Chinese old sayings. The character ma, a Chinese family name as with Mr. Ma, can also mean a horse. And old saying such as "An old horse knows its way around," or "Though taking a break in the stable, the old horse still wants to speed for thousands of miles." Apparently, Old Ma' Herbal Medicine Store was a well-chosen name for the business.

An old horse could also turn out to be a dark horse, and the lane prayed for his successful venture into the new line.

For all the blessing and firecrackers, concerns lingered in the lane. Those days, the majority of people still enjoyed the state medical insurance, and it did not appear so likely that they would come to a small private-run herbal drug store at their own expense, not to mention the fact that it took time to build up a customer base. Mr. Ma was already in his sixties.

But the lane got confused again. His business seemed to begin galloping ahead. Soon, visitors were seen lining up outside the herbal store. Mrs. Ma had to move out two wooden benches for the customers waiting outside.

Was it because of his expertise as a self-made doctor? An old horse, Mr. Ma might know his way among the herbs, but such popularity did not materialize overnight. The people in the lane could not help wondering. Foreigners, too, came to the herbal store—almost like in the old days of the bookstore. Perhaps there had been something suspicious going on there, one of his old neighbors said, to make the government put him behind bars in the sixties...

Finally, Old Root decided to take a closer look into the matter. Comrade Jun more than approved, even though it was no longer the age of the class struggle.

Old Root went to the store under the excuse of sending the Mas an urn of Shaoxin sticky rice wine. The wine was supposed to serve as a gesture of gratitude for the books he had read for free in the then bookstore.

That morning he found Mr. Ma's room furnished like a combination of a doctor's office and an herbal medicine store. Its white walls were lined with oak cabinets sporting numerous tiny drawers, each of them bearing a label for a particular herb, and in the midst, Mr. Ma sat at a mahogany desk, a white-haired, white-bearded man wearing silver-rimmed spectacles and a long string of carved beads—an immaculate image of a Taoist recluse enjoying longevity in harmony with nature. Beside the desk, a glass counter exhibited an impressive array of herb samples, along with unfolded books, magazines, and pictures, all illustrating the beneficial effects of the Oriental herbs.

There was a "foreign devil" too—a young girl with her long blond hair falling over her bare shoulders sitting in a chair opposite to Mr. Ma, her wrist like white jade shining on the mahogany desk.

"Let me take a look at your tongue."

Mr. Ma examined her tongue, nodded, and then pressed her wrist for pulse with his eyes closed.

"Nothing seriously wrong. The Yang appears slightly high at the expense of the Yin. So the energy does not flow in perfect harmony within your body. Maybe you have too much on your mind. I'm writing you a prescription, with some herbs for the Yin / Yang balance, and some for the blood circulation in the benefit of the whole system. Fresh herbs, I guarantee you."

"That's fantastic," the girl said in Chinese. "No way to get these fresh herbs in the United States."

Mr. Ma flourished a skunk-tail-blush pen over a piece of bamboo paper and handed the prescription to Mrs. Ma. "Choose the freshest herbs for her."

The business practice appeared truly impressive. The consolidation of handing out the prescription and herbs in one visit proved to be so convenient to the customers. But how could an American girl have learned of the herbal medicine store—in business in a lane for only two or three weeks?

"You're busy with your customers, Mr. Ma," Old Root said. "So I'm leaving the wine here. It's nothing, free from my nephew who now operates a wholesale chain of supplying Shaoxin sticky rice wine to hotels and restaurant. I'll come back when you are free."

But he waited outside the store. About five minutes later, the young American girl walked out with a large package in her hand, he approached her with the question.

"How have I learned of his business?" She said giggling. "Because of Dr. Zhivago!"

"What?" He was totally lost.

"You have read *Wenhui Daily*, haven't you? The thirtieth, last month."

So a copy of the *Wenhui Daily* came up on the desk of the neighborhood committee. Sure enough, the third page of it showed a special report entitled:

"Because of Doctor Zhivago"

Mr. Ma, an ordinary bookseller in Red Dust Lane, was thrown into prison in 1962—for the crime of having stored on the shelf a copy of *Doctor Zhivago* in English. It was then regarded as a counter-revolutionary book. Who the devil was Dr. Zhivago? A decadent bourgeoisie intellectual who tried to go against the red tide of the Russian revolution. As Chairman Mao said at the time, 'It's a new invention to write a novel in conspiracy against the Party." It certainly applied to Mr. Ma's shelving *Doctor Zhivago* too. The existence of the novel in the bookstore was reported to the Shanghai Police Bureau—along with the information that some bourgeois intellectuals regularly visited the bookstore, including a Rightist writer who had come back from the United State. So the charge was made, the bookstore was closed, and Mr. Ma was sentenced to thirty years in jail. He was allowed to carry inside with him only a Chinese medical dictionary. It was because Mao had said that Chinese medicine is a treasure.

Fortunately, it did not take thirty years for the Chinese translation of *Doctor Zhivago* to appear in our state-run bookstores. What the novel really is about, readers may have different opinions. But no one will take it as criminal evidence against a harmless bookseller. It took more than twenty years for Mr. Ma to get released. Five years less, thanks to our Party's new policy. Released and rehabilitated, Mr. Ma did not have the heart to reopen the bookstore. Instead, he tried to run an herbal medicine store with the knowledge acquired through his self-education from the one and only book available to him in prison. Presumably, he did not want that part of his life to be a total waste.

As an English proverb says, every black cloud has the silver lining. So because of *Dr. Zhivago*, Mr. Ma has become a doctor.

In the evening talk of the lane, Comrade Jun kept shaking his head over the article, unable to make a comment to the expecting audience.

"An article in *Wenhui Daily*!" Long-legged Pang said in the audience, "Old Ma surely has his connections. The publicity is worth a fortune."

"But how could the *Wenhui* reporter have learned of his story?" Four-eyed Liu asked.

It was a question none of them could answer. What kind of a man Doctor Zhivago was? Possibly a good doctor like Mr. Ma, who now started giving free herbs to his neighbors.

Not until about a month later did the lane come to learn another story from Four-eyed Liu, who got back in touch with an acquaintance connected with the *Wenhui Daily*.

A high-ranking police officer was said to have visited Mr. Ma's bookstore many years ago—perhaps a young man at the time, standing and reading there for free just like others. Now he heard the story about Mr. Ma, contacted the official in charge of "rectification of wrong cases," managed to have the old man released ahead of time.

The mysterious helper continued to look into his interest, going so far as to make sure that a special license was granted for the herbal medicine store. Whoever the cop was, he must have been a reader of *Doctor Zhivago*, so he told the story to his girlfriend, a young journalist in the *Wenhui Daily*. To humor him, she had the story published in the newspaper.

Old Root also learned something about the impossible relationship between the cop and the journalist, which was, of course, another story.

"It reminds me of another old Chinese story about horses," Old Root concluded. "When the old man of Sai lost his horse, it's not necessarily a bad thing, because the lost horse brought back another horse home in its company. There is no telling the causality of things in this world. Indeed, all because of Doctor Zhivago."

Overseas Chinese Lu

In narratology, there is a term called "unreliable narrator," unreliable because of the narrator's own interests involved. Usually, that refers to a character in the story, but the same can be applied to an author. For instance, while working on the Shanghai stories in the States, I may not have to worry about censorship or self-censorship that used to overwhelm me in China. But then what about marketing, timing, sales, reviews, and among so many other things, particularly about implied readers?

So what I'm going to tell you tonight is different. Here, in front of our Red Dust Lane, I don't have to worry as an author, but just as an ordinary man like you, with nothing better to do for the evening. If you like it, that's fine, but you may leave any time if it does not interest you. In short, I'm not worried.

Come to think about it, it's a true story that has been haunting me for years. But don't ask me to explain why, I really cannot—not even to myself. Telling it may just help a little, hopefully, like in psychoanalysis.

It's about Lu Tonghao, a friend of mine nicknamed Overseas Chinese. Lu used to live in an attic on Yan'an Road, close to Chenzhe Road, just a stone's throw way, but he occasionally stayed with his sister in Baokang Lane on the corner of Shandong and Ninghai Roads, almost as close.

Now the beginning of my middle school coincided with that of the Cultural Revolution in 1966, with the overwhelming humiliation of my father, a "capitalist" who had to endure the so-called revolutionary mass criticisms, wearing a blackboard around the neck as a "black monster," and having its dark shadow cast on the family as well. Struggling, nearly drowning in the waves of the revolutionary slogans such as "like father, like son, a black rat begets an equally black one capable of digging holes too," I was soon consumed with an inferiority complex, feeling like a sick, rotten egg.

In the midst of those slogans, I stepped into the middle school, Great Leap Forward on Sichuan Road. Those days, students in one neighborhood went to the same school. So Lu became my schoolmate, and then my friend.

It was perhaps not too surprising. Before 1949, my father had run a perfume company, and his father, a fur store. In the summer of 1966, his family, like mine, was ransacked and rummaged by Red Guards in the campaign of "Sweeping away the Four Olds"—the old ideas, old cultures, old conventions, and old habits—from the "black families." So both of us were subject to discriminations and humiliations as "black puppies" in school. Birds of a feather, so to speak.

But we were different. While I kept my tail humbly tucked in, Lu struck another pose, holding his head high, his hair mousse-shining. A "black puppy" he might have been, he's the one with the tail wagging in defiance. Far from feeling ashamed, Lu took an obstinate pride in his coming from that "good old family" of his, maintaining that his father "Ludwig" was the "white fox fur king" in the city. In contrast, I would have never dreamed of bragging and boasting of my father as "number one nose," though a true nickname in reference to his ability to determine the perfume quality. Still, we became close.

In school, Lu managed to openly cultivate "the decadent bourgeois taste"—brewing coffee, tossing fruit salad at home, and coming to school in a jacket made out of a western-style three-piece suit of his father's. And he did not even forget to make a point about its material imported from Italy.

That accounted for the origin of his nickname. "Overseas Chinese" was unmistakably a negative term those days, used figuratively to depict someone as unpatriotic, staying abroad, associated with the extravagant bourgeoisie life style in the western world.

Also, there was an unexpected incident contributing to the spreading of that nickname in school, where our reading was mostly of *Chairman Mao's Quotations*, and any other books were invariably condemned as politically incorrect. For instance, Guo Moru, then the number one official scholar and writer of the Party, declared all his previous books written before the Cultural Revolution were ideologically poisonous, let alone those by other writers. Millions and millions of copies were burned in public, libraries were closed, and nothing but the works by Mao were available in bookstores. But young people like us could not but be curious about the "poisonous books," so we managed to get hold of them by hook or by crook, and to read in stealth, sometimes under the red plastic cover of Chairman Mao's work.

At the beginning of the second school year, I succeeded in obtaining a Chinese translation of Dickens's *Hard Times* from my cousin. After devouring it overnight, I gave it to Lu, who promised to return it to me in one day. Because of that, he skipped school. Comrade Zhang, a member of the Mao Zedong Thought Propaganda Team at the school, made an unannounced visit to his home that evening, and caught him napping with the opened book beside. So Lu was supposed to plead guilty and confess about how he had gotten the book.

Once again, Lu proved to be so different, improvising on the spur of the moment, "Oh, this book I happened to find this morning in an old cardboard box at the neighborhood recycling center. Glancing through its preface, I lit on a statement made by Karl Marx, saying that Charles Dickens 'issued to the world more political and social truths than have been uttered by all the professional politicians, publicists, and moralists put together.' So I thought I, too, should study it."

For those translations published in the fifties or the sixties, a translator's introduction was a political must—in the invariable format of analyzing its narrative technique and criticizing its ideological tendency, and that with a relevant or not-that-relevant quote form Marx or Lenin. That served as the necessary political justification for its publication in China. So Comrade Zhang read the paragraph Lu pointed out for him— for three or four times, without being able to say anything.

"There were several other copies at the recycling center," Lu went on. "You may be able to find them if you hurry over there right now."

It could have been true, but there's no guarantee of any books left there after a long day.

"But the novel is not for you to read. Not for you, you impossible Overseas Chinese." Zhang too must have heard so much about his nickname

Hard Times was confiscated, but other than that, Lu stayed unscathed.

That saved my neck as well. I talked to Lu in gratitude, but he chose not to take any credit.

"Had I told Comrade Zhang the real story, it could have been a huge disaster for all the people involved. A student at another school caught in a similar situation, I've heard, was put into custody for weeks, as a suspect for the crime of running an underground network of exchanging western books."

In addition to the red-covered *Quotations of Chairman Mao* for us in school, we were also supposed to study the so-called newest and highest Mao instructions—whatever Mao had just said in the course of the Cultural Revolution. Shortly after the incident of *Hard Times*, Mao launched a nationwide campaign, declaring that "It is highly necessary for the educated youths to go to the countryside to receive reeducation from the poor and lower-and- middle class peasants." It had to be cheered and celebrated with drums and gongs as waves upon waves of "educated youths" were leaving the city for the reeducation. With just about one year before graduation, we found ourselves busy lining along the street, shouting slogans to see off the educated youths in red-flower-decked buses, squeezing into the railway station to salute the train pulling out of sight, feeling the siren that pierced the sky...

Again, Lu offered his different interpretations, kicking a pebble down to the rails.

"Educated youths? A crass joke! We have learned nothing in school. And what reeducation can the poor and lower-middle-class peasants possibly give us?"

Interpretation like that, if ever reported, could have landed Lu in serious trouble. Whatever Mao said must be absolutely correct. No one could ever question it. It was not until years later, with the Cultural Revolution officially declared as a well-meant mistake by Mao, did it come to light that he, having used the Red Guards to grab back his power in the mid-sixties, launched the campaign to get rid of them as educated youths for consolidation of his power in the late sixties.

One afternoon, after seeing off another group of the educated youths in a train rumbling toward the dismal distant horizon, I fell silent. Soon, others would be seeing us leaving the city like that. As we were dragging ourselves out of the suddenly deserted station, Lu murmured,

"Let's eat."

"What?"

"How long do you think we can enjoy the delicacies in this city of ours?"

He did not have to say more. In those poor, backward villages, the educated youths were said to be unable to keep the wolf from the door. According to Lu's elder brother Tongqing, who had left for Anhui Province earlier, having worked there for a whole year, he ended up make nothing but a pile of dried sweet potato. So it was just like Lu to emphasize on the importance of seizing the day.

I nodded, recalling the two lines composed by Cao Cao, a Han dynasty politician thousands of years earlier, "*Oh to sing over cups and dishes—/ how many times like that you have in life?*" Ironically, I learned the lines from a Japanese villain in "The Story of the Red Lantern," a revolution modern model Beijing opera, one of the few operas available to people for political education.

With the little pocket money, we contented ourselves pointing at the old brand restaurant windows, imagining, reminiscing, and occasionally, stepping into an inexpensive eatery. Again, it was up to Lu to lecture on proper appreciation of food in connection with the memories of the good old days. He made a point of ferreting out the original restaurant names. A western-styled bakery on Nanjing Road, for instance, was then called, "Workers, Farmers, and Soldiers," which made sense in that the bakery, like anything else, was supposed to serve the working class people first and foremost. But for Lu, such a name lent nothing to a gourmet's imagination. So he spared no pain elaborating on its pre-Cultural Revolution German name, *Kaisiling*, as if that name alone could have made a world of difference. Believe it or not, the cake we shared that day actually proved to be much richer in its creamy taste.

"The name is absolutely essential. Confucius says: 'There's nothing you can do or can be without a proper name,'" Lu insisted emphatically. "Chairman Mao says, '*Drinking the water from the Yangtze River,/ I am savoring the fish from Wuchang.*' The Wuchang fish truly tastes so much tender."

The lines about the Wuchang fish part actually came from a Mao poem we had studied in our textbook, but it was a poem in which Mao bragged and boasted about the distance of his swimming in Yangtze River. It's surprising that Lu would have applied it in the present context. Perhaps there's something in his nickname after all.

A couple of weeks later, Tang Deqiang, another schoolmate of ours, Lu, and I, set out together to the Old City God's Temple Market for a gastronomic campaign to "wipe out" all the eateries there. Following a much-discussed tactics, we tried to sample and share everything, a tiny bite or sip for each of the specials: chicken and duck blood soup, radish-shred cake, shrimp and meat dumplings, beef soup noodles, Nanyang soup buns, fried bean curd and vermicelli... Halfway through the ambitious campaign, much to our chagrin, that joint fund of ours ran out, and we had to beat a retreat. For some inexplicable reason, Tang no longer mixed with us afterward, but that failed venture in the Old City God's Temple Market never faded in my memory.

Before too long, it was our turn, as anticipated, to leave for the countryside. In spite of his protests in private, Lu set out to join his brother Tongqing in Anhui. Now, you may well say Lu did not have to go if he did not want to. But things were not like that at the time. For one, Old Hunchback Fang, an activist in the neighborhood committee, would come as the head of the propaganda team marching around the neighborhood, shouting through the loudspeaker under Lu's window to the heart-shuddering noise of drums and gongs, and that for two or three times a day.

"How can you try to stay behind in the city against Chairman Mao's great strategy, Lu? You have to leave for the countryside as an educated youth! For an educatable young man like you, you cannot choose your family background, but you still can choose your own road in the socialist China. "

"Educatable" was another political epithet then referring to "black puppies" like Lu and I, who might still be educated in spite of our black family background. The campaign brought a lot of pressure to bear upon us.

Whether lucky or unlucky, I happened to be suffering from an attack of acute bronchitis, which provided me with a ready excuse to remain in the city for a short while, but after recovery, I was still supposed to go to the countryside like others. Consequently, I turned into a "waiting-for-assignment youth"—another newly-coined term for young people waiting in limbo.

So began a difficult and long period for me. Out of school, out of work, with my schoolmates and friends all gone to the far- away countryside, I had no idea what to do with myself, alone in the city of Shanghai, waiting with no light visible at the end of the long tunnel.

In less than two months, however, Lu came back, tanned, thinned, but otherwise unchanged.

"It's simply absurd," Lu said, carrying for me a brown paper bag of peanuts from Anhui. "For a year's back-breaking toil and moil in the field, Tongqing gets nothing but two sacks of dried sweet potatoes. How can you possibly hope to live on that? In your splendid spring and autumn dreams! Their starved stomachs rumbling, the educated youths depend on the monthly packages and money order from Shanghai for survival."

The self-justification was made in an abated voice. As his brother remained there, working on the "special relationship" with the Party secretary of the village, Lu had no problem sneaking back to Shanghai, baby-sitting for his sister, and visiting me frequently. He sometimes carried over in his arms his little nephew named Luyi—the same as Louis in Chinese pronunciation, which Lu would enunciate with a deliberate touch of foreign accent. A docile toddler, the little Louis would play aside with toys in his own world of imagination.

Like in the school days, Lu liked to dwell on the mouth-watering delicacies, imagined or otherwise, in even more elaborated ways, such as the unbelievable "Buddha's head" consisting of a sparrow stuffed inside a quail stuffed inside a pigeon stuffed inside a white gourd, as the legendary "eye-goggling fish platter" featuring the carp fried with an ice cube in its mouth for just a second in the wok and served with its eyes still turning, as the variations of "the dragon fighting the tiger" with the material ranging from the rice paddy eel to the snake, or from the cat to the dog...With eight major schools of Chinese cuisine, Lu had a lot to lecture about, though he might not have tasted any of those fantastic dishes, I suspected, merely copying what he had heard or overheard. That made no difference to me. Waiting-for-recovery was now like a long tunnel stretching into infinity; I had to consider myself lucky because of Lu's regular visits.

For Lu, he could have made the visits for a necessary change of the scene from the chicken-cage-like the attic, in which he stayed with his parents. His family had been driven out of their large apartment at the beginning of the Cultural Revolution, and put in two places. One for his parents, an attic on Yan'an Road, and the other, a wing room for his sister's in Baokang Lane, which was not large, either.

For a visit to Lu, on the other hand, I had to shout out his name at the foot of the dark, treacherous stairs, making sure of his whereabouts before climbing up. In the small attic, where Lu had to squeeze into an enclave dug into the wall for the night, he looked embarrassed with my failure to find a place to sit. As a result, it's more often than not that he came to see me.

My parents had mixed feelings about his visits—sometimes as many as three or four times a week. While aware of his company meaning a lot to me, they began to be uneasy about his talk, particularly with the inevitable emphasis on the vanished glories of the "good old days," which could bring trouble even for the listeners. Then they became more worried upon discovery of the other reason—perhaps the more important one—for his numerous visits.

It was for book exchange like in our school days, but it was now growing to be a regular, full-scale operation for us. With four or five "bad books" at home as a sort of capital, Lu threw himself into busy lending and borrowing. I did the same, working around with a Balzac, two Dickens, and a Goethe in my possession. But for young people like us, out of school, out of work, with twenty-four hours on our hand, these seven or eight books were far from enough.

So we had to move beyond. In spite of the red slogans shaking the sky of the Cultural Revolution, some of the Shanghai families still kept "black books" secretly at home, and in secret circulation too. With library circulation out of the question, people had to exchange books in their own ways with rules and regulations attached, and we soon learned how to join in the circles.

"We have these books as the capital, and we have to keep the capital in good use," Lu said, explaining how he exchanged through his circle of book mates for quick circulations. "For instance, *Hamlet* by Shakespeare from me for *Handsome Friend* by Maupassant from Qingguan, my book mate in Hongkou district, for a week. Not a single day more."

Therein came the trick. It was essential for Lu to finish *Handsome Friend* in one night, and then to give it to me for another night. But that might not be enough, for we had to further exchange for other books through our respective circles—as long as the *Handsome Friend* was returned to Qingguan by the end of the week. In the course of it, the book could have traveled back and forth for four or five times--for a Balzac from B, for a Thomas Man from C, for a Hemingway from D... It could be risky, so we had to secure the reliable people for a safe and secret network. Any glitch could wreck the whole process.

Consequently, Lu's frequent visits to me to ensure the smooth operation.

While his circle consisted of those with similar family background, on my side, I developed different and mixed contacts. For instance, *The Count of Mount Cristo* came from a senior Party official's daughter. The republication of the book resulted, unexpectedly, from Madam Mao's revenging herself like the hero in the novel, and declaring that it was a masterpiece, so the novel came to be reprinted in the middle of the Cultural Revolution, accessible only to the Party cadres at certain ranks. While those cadres might not have been interested in the so-called inside books, not so with their kids, who might could lend them out to others.

I managed to let Lu have *The Count of Mount Cristo*—in four volumes—for only two days. Lu returned it to me red-eyed, explaining, "I have to read overnight. My sister reads during the day as she works for the nightshift."

We also developed some special technique for carrying a book. I would tuck it underneath the armpit inside the jacket. Lu would put the book in the toddler bag with the milk bottle sticking out. No one would ever suspect anything.

But during one of his visits, a copy of *Othello* accidentally fell out of the toddler bag—in the company of my parents. With all the positive comments made by Marx about Shakespeare, *Othello* still could get us into trouble, my parents believed, exchanging worried glances among themselves. That night, I overheard their discussion about their plan to proclaim Lu as one not welcomed to our home.

Prior to their intervention, however, something else happened. My mother, a recipient of the "out-of-the-system pay" for her long sick leave, lost her nerves to go to her toothpaste factory to pick up the money. The pay was not only reduced in comparison to the ordinary worker, but it also came with the epithet "out-of-the-system" as an unmistakable indication of her black status. It became a too humiliating experience for her to go there, signing her name on the register with a guilt-laden pen, and hanging her head low to her colleagues. But the amount, however drastically diminished, was crucial to our family. No income came from my father who was not allowed to work because of his eye trouble. I was told to run the monthly errand for her. The people at the toothpaste factory did not know me, mother said. But I hesitated. They at least knew me as a black puppy.

"I, too, have been doing that for my father for months," Lu said, cutting in. "It's just a matter of two or three minutes in the factory, showing your parent's ID card, signing at the form, and getting the money. No one there will say anything to you. Don't worry. If you like, I can accompany you there."

The toothpaste factory was located at quite a distance. It took a bus, and then a trolley bus, to get there. Aware of my reluctance, my mother handed me fifty cents by way of bus fare, an amount more than enough for both Lu and me. It was so reassuring that Lu would keep me company, she said.

The monthly errand turned out not to be that terrible. In a cubicle near the factory entrance, I murmured "Mom is sick" to a gray-haired accountant, and she readily produced a worn envelope containing the out-of-system pay. That's all about it.

As we started toward the exit of the factory, Lu suddenly said, "Have you heard stories about those skillful pickpockets in the overcrowded bus?"

"Yes?"

"We might as well walk our way back home."

I nodded, thinking of the envelope in my pocket. So that's what we did that afternoon.

Along the way, Lu demonstrated his knowledge about the inexpensive yet delicious eateries scattered here and there in the city. He could also be quiet practical in his way. A portion of fried bun for ten cents near Huanghe Road, a bowl of three-yellow chicken congee for only three cents on Yunnan Road, and a golden sticky rice cake for five a bit further to the east...

Not exactly to my surprise, I found my parents more tolerant toward Lu's visits afterwards. And I happened to overhear them discussing that it might not be a too bad idea for me to read, particularly when I had no idea about what to do with myself.

For the next trip, Lu and I saved more by walking there and back. It's a change that would soon enable us to start something like a budget gourmet adventure, Lu calculated.

"I know a place that serves super fried pork buns, inexpensive but fantastic, the best in the city," he said in high spirits. "Rujia, who came back from Hong Kong last week, went there directly the very next day. Lot of soup in the bun, unbelievable, she said."

About Rujia, I knew nothing except that she was a friend of the Lu's, having moved over to Hong Kong several years earlier. For Lu, that seemed to be enough to serve as an endorsement, as if her Hong Kong residency alone spoke volumes for the eatery. In spite of all the proletarian propaganda about hard working and simple living in the Party tradition, Shanghainese had their way of enjoying nice things while maintaining to be politically correct. After all, it would not be counted as against the proletarian spirit for people to have a portion of four fried buns for no more than ten cents.

The eatery was tucked in a side street behind New China Cinema. Sure enough, there was a long line of "budget-gourmets" waiting outside, shivering against the winter wind, smelling at the tantalizing mixture of chopped scallion and white sesame on top of the tiny buns, and listening to the impatient sizzle as the chef threw in a cup of water to the large cast-iron pan. It's definitely worth it, Lu declared, to wait for a couple of hours. Rubbing his hands, he started telling me about the secret recipe for the miraculous soup in the bun.

"People have to boil pork skin for hours, sometimes overnight, into something like jelly, which then is mixed into the ground pork stuffing. When the buns are being fried in the wok, the jelly melts into soup. And you know what? When Chaplin visited China in the thirties, he was so surprised with the soup squirting out of the bun. The Hollywood star devoured three portions of them at one setting."

I wondered whether it was a true story. When our turn finally came, I hastened to stuff a crisp-bottomed bun into my mouths like the Hollywood star. The hot soup burst out against my palate with a heavenly sensation, producing one of those moments surprisingly memorable in the Cultural Revolution, and leaving blisters on my lips for days.

"Let's go to Park Hotel today," Lu said on the fourth or fifth time that we emerged out of the factory, snapping his fingers for emphasis. "Park Hotel. In the hotel lobby, there's still a counter selling French bakery. My treat today."

"Park Hotel?"

"Well, it's called International Hotel nowadays. That does not make any sense. But the old bakery chef there is really extraordinary, trust me, who has worked in London."

I did not know where he gained all the information, but we made a detour to the hotel in question, the then highest building in the city, overlooking People's Park majestically across Nanjing Road. I had never stepped into the grand hotel before, but Lu carried himself casually like at home. Whistling, he settled on a long French loaf as well as a bottle of brown-colored drink called *Shashi*.

"The taste is really close to Coca," he poured me half a cup before taking a leisured sip for himself. Coca-Cola sounded like a far-away wonder, a brand symbolic of American imperialism. In fact, the knowledge of its existence came, thanks to the miraculous Chinese translation, *kekokele*, which means delicious and enjoyable, and at the same time sounds almost the same as in the English original. But *Shashi* tasted more like cough medicine, in spite of Lu's assurance. I had a hard time swallowing it.

It was not that often, fortunately, for us to visit a grand place like Park Hotel. But instead of grabbing snacks at the street booths, we started to save for inexpensive yet tasty meals, such as lamb hot pot in Hongchangxing, pork steak at Eastern Sea, three-yellow chicken at Little Shaoxin. As always, Lu made a point of introducing and explaining those time-honored specials to me.

In the midst of our gastronomy adventures, we managed to go on with the other one, that of our book exchange.

Among the books from Lu, one was *Jean-Christophe* by Roman Rolland, a story about a young man struggling his way up against all the odds, and I was deeply touched. At that time, the very concept of self-improvement was politically incorrect. People were supposed to function themselves like selfless screws fastened on the state machine. It's all determined by the Party, and in the interests of the Party too. But the young protagonist of the French novel made me think hard. I must have read it two or three times. Lu too liked it, citing one passage in particular about Jean-Christophe being treated by his fans to a sumptuous meal with southern French specials in rich creamy sauces.

At the beginning of my third "waiting for recovery" year, I took a neighbor's suggestion to practice tai chi at Bund Park in the morning. It was said to be helpful to bronchitis, but there I switched to English study by myself sitting on a green bench close to the bank. It was a change possibly prompted with the worries about the future, with the sight of a young girl studying on a green bench under the willow shoots, and with the story of Jean Christophe still so fresh in mind. He overcomes the odds. What about me?

Lu was unable to go there with me, having to babysit his nephew, he explained in earnest, too busy in the early morning. He cracked a joke about my motive when I told him about the mysterious disappearance of the young girl on the green park bench.

Anyway, the time I spent in the park was getting longer. Back home, the invariable sight of my parents huddling together, sick and depressed, more than disheartened me. The park provided a much-needed change of the scene. A white gull occasionally came soaring overhead, as if with elusive message shimmering in the green foliage.

Because of my setting out early, in imitation of an old proverb of "practicing the sword with the first cock's crow," my mother encouraged me with some breakfast money, not much, only ten cents a day, but quite a sum to me those days.

"It's better for him to go out studying than to sit at home worrying," she said to my father.

For a common Shanghai breakfast, an earthen oven cakes with a fried dough stick, it cost only seven cents, so I managed to save a bit more by having just a cake, or skipping the meal. That way, I soon would be able to indulge myself gastronomically again in the company of Lu.

But some other things were also changing. After President Nixon's recent visit to China, the *People's Daily* chose to quote Marx, saying that "the command of foreign languages can be an important weapon in one's life." And in the old book section of the Shanghai Foreign Language Bookstore, people could occasionally find one or two useful reference books. Four-eyed Ling, a veteran bookseller, handed me books like *Advanced Lerner's English Dictionary* hidden under the counter, which certainly helped with my English study, but made a dent on my budget.

During the period, Lu went to the Anhui village for a couple more times. Like before, his brother Tongqing had been taking care of things for him there. So the main purpose of his trips was to bring gifts from Shanghai to the village Party secretary, who made sure of his name being kept on the "commune work point register," as if he had been working there just like other educated youths, "receiving reeducation from the poor farmers."

But that's what I guessed, he did not tell me too much about it. I, too, was busy with my own things. I further expanded my "book exchange operation," though in the changed circumstances and methods, with books in English.

While I did not have any English novels to exchange with, I learned that a different group of people might help—the English teachers in schools and colleges. It was possible for them to teach English again, but only with such slogans as "Long live Chairman Mao," or "Down with American imperialism." For their books at home, they were not supposed to let young people read or know. Again, thanks to my mother's breakfast money, I was able to approach them by behaving like an ancient young student—carrying shuxiu which Confucius meant to be presents like ham or dried meat in place of tuition. Among the English book owners, one was a middle-aged middle school teacher named Zhumei, who reminded me of Lu, especially with his reminiscence of the old days over a cup of wine, except that Zhumei was more resigned, more realistic. I was lucky enough to get some difficult-to-get liquor for Zhumei through a friend working in a wine shop. Zhumei liked it so much, allowing me full access to his bookshelf.

To my own surprise, it did not take too long to find myself starting to struggle through novels in English, skipping the words and phrases not really known to me, and guessing and imagining through the context. The water lapping against the shores of Huangpu River, those books were opening a brave new world to me.

From an English novel titled *Random Harvest*, I picked up an argument I found particularly relevant to Lu and me. The hero, a soldier in the First World War falling prey to a counter-intelligence setup, questions its justification as he lies wounded moaning deliriously in the trench. The trap appears logical for the sake of winning the war, but what about the victims sent unknowingly into the setup?

"Is it fair for black puppies like us to be singled out as the sacrifice for the Cultural Revolution?" I said to Lu, holding the book.

He nodded without making a direct response, and said he had heard about a Hollywood movie based on the novel. "There's a fantastic Chinese translation of its title, *Reunion of Mandarin Ducks*. Mandarin ducks are symbolic of inseparable lovers in traditional Chinese literature, you know."

He surely knew a lot about things in the old Shanghai. Still, I enjoyed a sense of advantage over Lu, reading in English as well as in Chinese. But Lu did not grudge me that. He surprised me with a hard-covered copy of *Three Musketeers* in English.

"I found the book used as a sort of placemat under the rice pot in a neighbor's home. I got it in exchange, believe it or not, for a fried sticky rice cake. So it's yours to keep."

In 1974, my waiting-for-recovery period came to an abrupt end. I was suddenly told to work in Shenzhe Neighborhood Production Group because of Mao's latest and highest instruction in a letter that "there are problems with the movement of the educated youths going to the countryside." The admission came in response to people's widespread complaining. With such a gesture made, Mao remained one hundred percent correct, and his letter further demonstrated his profound concern for the Chinese people. So there's no point, apparently, in people like me waiting any longer. But what then? The national economy collapsed, no job opening in the state-owned companies. A neighborhood production group, more like a community co-op in reality, with less pay and no medical benefit, became a sort of solution. Since we were not those educated youths who had passionately followed Mao's call to the countryside, we could hardly complain about the poor-paid job.

Working three-shift in the neighborhood production group, making hats and gloves on the ancient sewing machine streamline, I struggled not to give up my English studies, but I had less and less time for other things, including that of dining out with Lu like before.

What about the future? "*When young, we knew nothing about worries, / for the sake of a poem, we had a hard time mouthing worries.*" I tried to translate Song dynasty poet Xin Qiji's lines into English.

But Lu was a man with his own opinion. He believed that things would soon change for the better, whispering to me over a bowl of shrimp dumplings, tapping a tune on the sidewalk littered with shrimp peels and fish bones, and stirring up the scallion-strewn soup with a long, optimistic spoon of his.

"Soon a new government policy will come out about the compensation for families like ours—for the loss suffered during the 'sweeping away four olds' campaign, you know. It's huge, I've heard."

With the Red Guards out of Mao's favor, Mao came to think that their once "revolutionary activities" had better be seen in a new light. So compensation became a topic whispered about in the circle. Regarding the possibility of any substantial sum, however, I was not sure. My father being sick, I turned into the family representative to discuss with the "revolutionary committee" of his company about the compensation. According to the committee, more than half was missing from what had been taken away from our home that night. Besides, the way the sum was calculated was so characteristic of the Cultural

Revolution. The jewelries, for instance, were estimated in accordance to the estimated total weight—about two handfuls—then at the rate of 99 yuan for 50 grams. As a result, the compensation amount was a joke. Lu appeared to be far more optimistic, though.

The government policy eventually came into effect. "It calls for a celebration," Lu declared in high spirits. I did not know how to respond. It was nothing to talk about for my family, but for Lu's, it's possibly a different story. As if anxious to prove it, he invited me to East Wind Restaurant on the Bund.

"You know the history of this place? The magnificent British building stood on the corner of the Bund and Yan'an Road as early as the late Qing dynasty. It used to be the celebrated Shanghai Club boasting of the longest bar with the most immaculate service in Asia. After 1949, the Communist government turned it into International Seamen's Club. It has now become East Wind Restaurant. Whatever the change in name, it's a fantastic place. Oh, imagine my father smoking a Cuban cigar here with his business associates in the glories of the good old days."

The red-brick grand restaurant seemed to be well-chosen, at least in association with the "good old days." Lu brought Louis along with him. In a year or two, Louis would go to primary school, but he followed Lu around with expectation written in his large eyes. That evening, the dining hall turned out to be too noisy, too overcrowded for any decent service. I failed to see the historical bar, which must have been removed at the beginning of the Cultural Revolution. We seated ourselves at a soy-sauce-stained table, settling on a couple of not-too-expensive dishes, as well as a large bowl of mandarin fish soup chosen by Louis, who kept rolling his curious eyes toward a large water tank in a corner near the entrance, waiting for the waiter to ladle out the swimming fish. He was disappointed, seeing no one move close to the tank after we gave the order.

It took a while before the soup was placed on the table. Lu lost no time introducing to me the "secret recipe" of the soup.

"Look at the soup. Absolutely milky white! But it's easy. You just have to wok-fry the live fish first, add chicken and ham broth, and then let it simmer over very small fire for hours. When the soup finally turns white, you throw in a handful of pepper and scallion before serving it steaming hot to the table."

The fish soup tasted delicious, the meat tender, almost transparent white against the chopped green onion and sliced red pepper. Helping myself to another spoonful, I hastened to make a mental note of the recipe in the midst of his satisfied burps.

"We'll come here again," he said in great confidence, "with more compensations rolling in for good families like ours. Another celebration dinner, for sure, in a fancier restaurant."

I was not so sure whether it could be sustainable for us to go on squandering on imagined compensations in the future.

It was coincidental that night, while browsing through a biography about William James, I picked up a metaphor for pragmatism. It's about a long corridor lined with a number of rooms, of different shapes and sizes, where a man pushes open a door by chance, and then chooses to stay inside since he finds it comfortable. Staring at the sleepless ceiling, where water stains remained discolored stains without changing into any fanciful patterns at night, I had an unshakable feeling that Lu and I must have checked into different rooms.

Shortly after that dinner, Lu made another trip to Anhui. The treat he had promised so emphatically never materialized. But that did not bother me. Perhaps there came no more compensation as he had expected, perhaps he failed to find a fancier restaurant.

Toward the end of 1975, it seemed as if out of the blue, Lu got a job at a state-rung shipping company in Anhui Province, stationed on a small cargo boat along Huai River with the possibility of occasionally sailing back into Huangpu River, Shanghai. In the light of Mao's theory for the movement of "educated youths," it was necessary for them to get reeducated in the countryside, but not necessarily to stay there forever as farmers, so for some of them, after receiving "successful reeducation," they would be given jobs in local companies.

"But you have spent most of the time in Shanghai—for your reeducation!" I said in confusion.

"It's really up to the village head to determines who has received successful reeducation or not. He's a buddy of Tongqing's, you know. At his recommendation, Tongqing has got an even better job--on the Anhui-Shanghai train."

Lu did not have to say any more. In spite of the slogans and propagandas of the Cultural Revolution, it was those in power that had the final say.

"It may not be a large boat," Lu added, "with only three or four people on board, but with possible free trips back to Shanghai, I really cannot complain. And it's a state-owned company."

So it was a good, even enviable position, compared with other educated youths assigned to work in the local mines or commune factories.

"I'll treat you to a free ride along the river," he went on, "drinking coffee and smoking cigars and looking out to the magnificent buildings along the Bund like in a movie in the thirties."

Lu never invited me to his boat, though. Nor did I succeed in juxtaposing the image of a sweaty boatman washing off the deck to that of an overseas Chinese whistling a serenade along the river, stirring his fantasy in a coffee cup. But I could have been too exhausted on the electronic sewing machine, stitching out circles and circles, blindly, on the soles of labor protection boots. One late night shift, I got my sleepy finger pierced by the needle. Afterward, while trying to console myself with a lone bowl of beef soup noodles in a shabby eatery, I realized I had not seen Lu for more than half a year.

In the midst of all this, the Cultural Revolution came to a sudden ending with a wimp. Things began returning to the pre-revolution order and practice. For one, the college entrance test in 1977, through which I entered East China Normal University with a high score in English, thanks to those mornings in Bund Park.

Shortly afterward, I started my graduate study in Beijing through a special MA program at Chinese Academy of Social Sciences, majoring in English and American literature. I studied under Professor Bian Zilin, who was already in his seventies, quite frail at the time, so I went to his home instead of the classroom once or twice a week. More of a poet than anything else, Bian would sometimes talk to me about his conceiving the lines on a donkey, or writing a novel in English at a London apartment in the late forties, when he changed his mind and came back to China for the socialist revolution, tossing the incomplete manuscript into fire as something bourgeois and decadent.

"But for the brainwashing," I contemplated, thinking of Lu again, "Bian could have remained there as an overseas Chinese, writing bestsellers."

For the next three years, I was able to come back to Shanghai only during Chinese New Year holidays, but Lu's boat seemed to be invariably busy, stationed so far away. At least that was the impression to me.

For the third or fourth visit to his home, I still failed to see him. I left several books with his mother, who offered me a bag of brown sugar sticky rice cake in the holiday celebration, saying Lu insisted on giving it to me, the cake made in accordance to his own recipe, with the special sticky rice brought back from Anhui. It stuck to my teeth, but otherwise not that special.

After graduation in Beijing, I came back to work in the Shanghai Academy of Sciences as an associate researcher professor. The job consisted of translating poems and stories from English into Chinese, and writing the "translator introduction" by quoting Marx or Lenin, like the piece that had once saved Lu's neck in our middle school days. The eighties happened to be a period described as the "golden ten years for modern Chinese poetry." In addition to translating Eliot and Yeats, I also started writing poems, and obtained the membership of the Chinese Writers' Association.

Lu too seemed to be so busy, trying to have himself transferred back to Shanghai. In the early and mid-eighties, most of the educated youths had returned to the city with the movement of their going to the countryside written off as part of the Cultural Revolution. In contrast, the boat job of his in Anhui was no longer seen as something enviable.

What's more, while a number of the "good families" welcomed back their overseas relatives and friends in great fanfare, nothing like that seemed to have ever happened to the Lus. In the ever-changing Chinese language, "Overseas Chinese" now turned into a positive term in associations with wealth and opportunities from the west. That must have added to his pressure. In the meantime, he started dating a young girl of an ordinary family, working at a candy store on Yan'an Road, but for someone like him with neither a job in Shanghai, nor a room under his name, it was something seen to his credit to have a "Shanghai girlfriend."

One late May afternoon, I went to see Lu with a copy of Conrad's novellas, including *Secret Sharer* translated into Chinese by me. In the course of the translation, I had somehow thought of Lu in parallel to the mysterious "other" in the story. That afternoon, Lu was with his girlfriend nicknamed Oriole in a partitioned-out enclosure in his sister's backroom, dark, windowless, with just enough space for a bed. They were sitting on the edge of the bed, and I, on a chair pulled in for my visit. A sweet girl, Oriole kept putting sugar-covered walnuts in a dish on top of Conrad on the bed, a syrup stain on her forefinger.

"From my store, free," she repeated, flashing a smile against the peeling wall.

That seemed to be about all I remembered of that visit. I left the book behind without bringing up the topic of its relevance. Neither Lu nor Oriole asked me anything about it. Not a single word about the translation.

A couple of month later, unexpectedly, Lu paid a visit to me in my office. The building of the Shanghai Academy of Social Sciences was located on Central Huaihai Road. It housed several other institutions, including the editorial office of *Democracy and Legal System*, a then influential magazine connected to some people at the top. As it happened, I got acquainted with Ershi, a journalist of the magazine, who liked telling me the "inside information" about the political maneuverings behind high-profile criminal cases, and I gave him a couple of my books. He then surprised me by producing a profile about my work in *Wenhui Daily*. It was because of that article, which Lu had read, he came to me with a specific request.

Lu wanted me to forward a petition to the city government through Ershi. According to it, Lu's father Ludwig had purchased a villa in Jing'an District in early 1949, but wary of the possible trouble under the new Communist regime, Ludwig played safe by registering the property under his brother's name. Sure enough, it spared him trouble—at least in that aspect—for the subsequent years. In the mid-eighties, people found it politically safe to talk about private property again, but his brother refused to return it to the rightful owner. Ludwig's argument, while probably true, was not backed by any evidence. So Lu thought of me, seeing in my connection with Ershi a possibility to turn the table. I agreed to forward it, though pretty sure that a journalist like Ershi was in no position to help.

Nothing seemed to come out of Ershi's effort, as anticipated. Lu chose not to pressure me for it, but I saw him even less afterward, what with his boat being away, and with his having to seize the time to see his girlfriend in Shanghai...

Toward the end of 1988, I got a Ford Foundation fellowship for a year of research in the United States. I contacted Washington University in St. Louis, considering it a good opportunity for me to do research on T. Eliot in his home city, and then to write a book about him back in China.

Before leaving, I went to see Lu. That morning, Lu was squatting in the dark space under the staircase, making coal briquettes with the coal dust purchased at a discount from the neighborhood store. Stripped to his waist, his face sweaty, smeared, he looked like anything but an overseas Chinese. Wiping his black hands in vain on a gray apron, he took me upstairs, where Oriole was busy making egg skin dumplings over a small stove, an embodiment of a virtuous wife. They had married a short while earlier.

What we talked about that day, I barely remembered, except the point he made about the special dumplings.

"It takes a lot of patience and skill to produce the egg skin in a tiny ladle, and then to wrap it over the pork stuffing really carefully without breaking. But there's nothing like homemade egg skin dumplings with a lot of pork skin jelly mixed in the stuffing. Remember the mini fried buns behind the movie theater, don't you? This tastes even better. You definitely should try her cooking today."

"Lu has taught me all this," She said, looking up at him, her large eyes full of admiration. "He knows such a lot."

The egg skin dumplings proved to be extraordinarily delicious. Usually, they come in a pot of soup, just three or four of them on top along with vegetables or transparent noodles, but that day, I had a large bowl of the fresh-made egg skin dumplings, perhaps more than twenty pieces. Oriole kept looking on nervously, lest I failed to do it justice. I stuffed myself.

Finally, as I stood up to leave, Lu said in a subdued voice,

"Don't forget us."

"How? I'll be back in just a year."

"Well, we'll see," he said, tapping a cigarette. "An overseas—"

In the then movies and magazines, most of the Chinese, once abroad, chose to stay on and eventually, as overseas Chinese. That was not my plan, but I saw no point arguing about it with him.

I left for the United States as planned, carrying the research outline for the Eliot project. It would be quite a fulfilling year, I believed.

Indeed, like in an ancient proverb, eight or nine times out of ten, things do not go the way planned. Before one year was over for my research project, the crackdown at Tiananmen Square in Beijing happened. To my consternation, I was mentioned in the Voice of America as "a Chinese poet hawking spring rolls in charity sales in St. Louis for the students in China" --with the recipe learned from Lu, incidentally. The next day, people in the Shanghai Police Bureau contacted my sister Xiaohong, wanting her to tell me to behave myself. Then the publisher in Guiling wrote me that the publication of my poetry collection was cancelled, even though I was already through with the proof. All the messages were unmistakable.

I had no choice, I realized, but to stay on at Washington University. I decided to study there for a Ph. D. degree, which was necessary for my visa status, and to switch to writing in English as I could no longer publish in China. Thanks to the professors at the university, I was encouraged to take a number of courses in the creative writing program while working on a Ph. D. thesis in comparative literature. I began publishing in English in the meantime. One of my poems at the time won a prestigious prize in the Missouri State.

What can be recaptured in memory if one /got lost then and there? Master Zhuang awakes / wondering if it is he who dreamed / of being a butterfly, or it is / a butterfly that dreams of being / Master Zhuang. Now the zoom...zoom / of the dryer she applying to her hair / after the bath, or the distant sound / guns the soldiers are firing / among the people in the square. / I begin making decisions: to go into exile, / not to compromise on the Chinese original, / to do justice to Li Shangyin. And she / comes to bed, turning off the light.

For the next five or six years, I was too busy, also too nervous, to go back to China. It was still in the pre-email period for me. I lost contact with most of my old friends, including Lu. The last thing I wanted to do was to cause them any trouble. In the few cautious letters from Shanghai, my sister never mentioned Lu.

I began to feel more and more nostalgic, among other things, missing particularly those gastronomic adventures in the company of Lu. Perhaps it's like in *Remembrance of Things Past*, with the new meanings emerging out of recollection.

But more often than not, it was for a reason surprising to myself. In St. Louis, Chinese restaurants were mostly Americanized. In a parody to a patriotic song, "Nothing can change our Chinese hearts," people liked to say instead, "Nothing can ever change the Chinese palate." So I tried to cook at home with the memories of those days with Lu crowding back.

Some of the recipes from Lu helped more than I had imagined, especially in the month after the birth of our daughter. According to a time-honored Chinese tradition, the new mother is supposed to lie on bed for a whole month and enjoy all the delicacies imaginable, including a conventional southern must—crucian carp soup with Jinhua ham. That posted a challenge to me. Neither crucian carp nor Jinhua ham available in the St. Louis market, I chose butter fish and smoked pork shank instead, but I strictly followed the soup-making steps Lu had instructed in the Bund restaurant. Sure enough, the soup turned out to be appealingly white and delicious, which earned me a rare compliment from my wife as "the best fish soup ever tasted."

Time flows away like water, with fish-like shadows rippling occasionally in the memories of the sleepless night.

In 1996, I made the first trip from St. Louis back to Shanghai. The city had been changing so dramatically. A lot turned out to be unrecognizable to me. So with the people there. I asked my sister about Lu.

"He's not come to visit us since you left. Not for a single time," she said with an undisguised note of disapproval. "But he could have moved away. I've not seen him around for quite a while. The last time I saw him riding an old bike across Shandong Road was, let me think, about two or three years ago."

The next afternoon, I set out to that attic of his on Yan'an Road, but the *shikumen* house had disappeared, with a subway exit in construction visible not far away from there. I then went to his sister's in Baokang Lane. She was still in there, and she told me that Lu had moved back to the city of Shanghai, now having his own apartment in Yangpu District, and working at Duhongfang, a delicatessen close to the intersection of Xizhuang and Yan'an Roads.

"Oh he's a manager now," she added in afterthought as I started groping downstairs, like years earlier, in the dark.

Duhongfang was an old-brand delicatessen known for its red braised pork, smoked fish head, salted duck wings, among others. It took me less than ten minutes to arrive in sight of the glass counter facing the street, displaying the old brand braised pork shining red and rich in the afternoon light like before, except the counter seemed to be much smaller.

I stepped in to an unexpected scene of shabbily-clothed customers huddling over bowls of dumplings behind the delicatessen section, talking loudly in their dialects, smoking, laughing, and smacking their lips. According to the blackboard menu on the wall, the dumpling appeared to be rather inexpensive, and the number of customers there spoke for its popularity.

Lu was there, wearing an oil-smeared uniform, moving to clear a table with a wet mop in his hand. He was startled at the nickname I called out like in the old days,

"Overseas Chinese Lu!"

"You—" He turned round with a start, blinking before recognition hit home, tongue-tied.

"After all these years," I said, grasping for his hand he was wiping on the uniform, "so much for us to catch up. Let's go to a quieter place, Lu. A fancy restaurant. How about Park Hotel? My treat. It's already four thirty."

"How about having a bowl of dumpling first?" he said hesitantly, not in a hurry to go. "I'm the afternoon manager here. My shift does not finish until six thirty."

"That's fine. Let's talk here, but—"

Lu led me to a table tucked in behind the cardboard-like partition wall, close to the kitchen, in a small area reserved for the employees. I could hear something sizzling in oil in the kitchen, smelling like salted belt fish.

Lu sat opposite at the table. But it was not really like Lu, who would have jumped at the dinner suggestion at a fancy place like Park Hotel. For a state-run store manager, it would have not mattered, I supposed, to leave one or two hours earlier with a friend he had not seen for so many years.

"The best dumplings," Lu shouted in a loud voice to the kitchen, "for my old friend back from the United States."

So we started chatting over the dumplings with mixed pork and shepherd purse blossom stuffing, with ginger and egg slices strewn generously over the soup, a scene so familiar in our school days.

What had happened to him those years, however, seemed not to be interesting enough to make a story, as he launched into a narrative. At the beginning of the nineties, with the movement of the reeducation for educated youths officially acknowledged problematic, the ex-educated youths were allowed back to the city. Giving up his boat job, he too managed to return riding the tide and got a job here. After working as a salesman for several years at the front counter, he was now serving as a shift manager.

"In short, not at the top, not at the bottom. After all, so many people are laid off in today's Shanghai..."

And his narrative was punctuated by the salesgirl shouting out questions to him from the front counter, and by the chef from the kitchen asking for a cigarette in return for the free dumplings. Lu had to rise from the table and to move back and forth. It was a job that kept him on the run.

"Duhongfang is one of the celebrated old brands in the city," he said, stirring the memories in his bowl. "During the Cultural Revolution, it was named Red East—"

"Yes, you told me about the origin of Red East, and joked about the store name coming from the red-colored pork, I still remember."

"Really!" He eyed me in confusion. "But delicatessens are going out of fashion, whatever names they may be called."

"How could that possibly be?"

"In the past, a Shanghai host would insist on treating his guests at home. Because of the shortage in food supply, and because of the limited number of restaurants, no more than two or three along the entire Xizhuang Road, a delicatessen could really help. But today, with so many restaurants around, the host would lose face without taking his guests out to a restaurant just one block or two away."

That's why there were few customers at the front counter in spite of its being an old brand. It had to serve dumplings in the back, I guessed, in compensation for the declining business. I spooned up another dumpling, the shepherd purse blossom inside still so deliciously green, which was seen as wild weed, inedible in that backyard of my American neighbor's.

"Changed, changed utterly," Lu said, concluding with a popular song coming out from a radio somewhere. "*Yesterday's dream is scattered by the wind, / but the wind is still dreaming of yesterday moon...*"

"Let's go to some other place after your shift. How about East Wind Restaurant on the Bund?" I suggested again, recalling that dinner years ago. There I might as well tell him about the success of the fish soup in the States.

"East Wind is long gone. It's been changed to Kentucky Fried Chicken, I noticed just the other day."

"Why?"

"Shanghainese consider KFC fancy, high-class. World-known, all the way from America, you know. Some fashionable people choose to have even their wedding parties there."

"Well, you pick a good restaurant then. You surely know a lot of them in the city. "

Still, Lu seemed not to be eager, murmuring that he was busy helping with her daughter doing homework in the evening, wiping his mouth again with a scrap of paper napkin. It came like a cue to me.

I rose to leave, following Lu through the cluster of tables toward the front door. Among the dumpling eaters, an odd customer was chewing slices of wine-immersed pig ear over a large cup of beer, possibly drunk, humming a tune to himself in a corner.

"Have you heard of Tang's story?" Lu said abruptly.

"Tang, what story?"

"He committed suicide four or five years ago, jumping into a deserted well. Starved to death. Undiscovered until weeks later. An educated youth in the far-away Jiangxi village, where the tractor he drove fell into a ditch. He never recovered. Something wrong in his head."

I thought of that long-ago afternoon, when Tang, Lu and I went in a "gourmet campaign" in the Old City God Temple Market, determined to taste each and every shabby eatery there, with the sunlight streaming into the youthful laughter of our absurd adventure…

Then two lines in Chen Yuyi's poem came back to me. *Twenty years has passed like a dream./ It is a wonder that I am still here*—still together with Lu.

In a flash of deja vu, I looked up across the street to the façade of the Big World, the once popular entertainment center of the city, now deserted, dust-covered in hopeless disrepair. The building had been originally designed with a number of halls and stages in the open, with no possibility of installing air conditioning or other modern facilities in a present-day renovation. In front of the building, in the early days of the movement of "educated youths going to the countryside," Lu and I had more than once stood there, waving our hands to the red-flower-decked buses rolling into the distance. Next to the chained-up entrance of the Big World, I saw a new Sichuan restaurant sporting a large neon sign "Drunken South." A lone blue jay was seen flickering around the neon in the late afternoon light.

"What about lunch tomorrow at Drunken South? Just across the street," I said. "You have lunch break, haven't you?"

"Twelve o'clock then," he said nodding. "I'll be waiting for you there."

The next noon I saw Lu sitting straight at a table near the entrance of the Sichuan restaurant, wearing a new blue blazer, a white silk handkerchief peeping out his breast pocket. A shadow of the once Overseas Chinese Lu still so vivid in memory, but out of place, oddly, in the shabby restaurant with young waitresses in the imitation indigo costume moving around, greeting in imitation Sichuan accent.

The moment I seated myself at the table, he said, pushing the menu across to me, "You choose. Now you've really seen the world. What a lucky man!"

"Well, whether the water feels cold or warm in the spring river, it is known only to the duck swimming in it." I chose not to elaborate about the luck part, evading with a paraphrased quote from the Song dynasty poet Su Dongpo, and picking up the dog-eared menu.

We each chose a couple of dishes, neither expensive nor exotic, but rather old-fashioned. Spicy beef tendon, fried frog legs in mini wok, Kung Pao chicken, Mala spicy tofu, in addition to a platter of catfish immersed in red pepper oil, which Lu recommended as the latest culinary fashion of the city.

The fish proved to be surprisingly tender, with its white meat shining through the spicy red sauce, and we had to constantly wash our palates with Qingdao beer. The frog legs enticing with dainty goji berries strewn around on a miniature stove, Sichuan beef tender looking transparent, crisp. Indeed these were the specials not imaginable in American restaurants.

Between the cups, I started narrating my experiment with the butter fish soup in St. Louis. He nodded, sipping at the beer, tearing a sinewy thigh from the frog, a vacant look in his eyes.

Then it was his turn to fill in the details here and there about his story he had told so quickly the previous day. With more than ten years wasted, it's tough for him to find a decent job upon returning to Shanghai. Checking "cooking" as his special skill in the application form, fortunately, secured him the job in the state-run delicatessen, and then the demolishing of his parents' attic in the housing reform of the city got him an efficiency room in compensation in Yangpu District.

"It's an old unit of one single oblong room, not like today's apartment consisting of a living room and a bed room, so I've partitioned the unit into two just like that," he said slowly, sticking his chopsticks into the eye of the fish, breaking the head open, as if in demonstration of the renovation project.

From his perspective, it's basically a tale of his still doing fine, though not necessarily a successful overseas Chinese with incredible luck—like me.

"As a genuine overseas Chinese, you know better," he said with a placid shrug of his shoulders, helping himself to another spoon of the fish soup, as if finally resigned to the reversal of our status in the restaurant.

A pretty young waitress, dressed in a sleeveless indigo blouse and shorts in the southern style, came flitting over light-footed to our table, her bare legs and ankles white and shining, like an illustration torn from a classic album, adding another Qingdao bottle on the table.

I was seized with a sort of disorientation, murmuring some half-forgotten lines in spite of myself. "*Shining brighter than the moon, / she serves from the wine urn, / her wrists dazzlingly white, like / frost, like snow. / Still young, I am not / going back home, or / I'll have a broken heart.*"

It was from a sentimental *ci* poem about the charms of the South written by the late Tang dynasty poet Wei Zhuang. In the ninth century, the South probably included the present-day Shanghai. I was trying to bring our talk back to the books we had read in the earlier days.

"But we are no longer young," Lu said, picking up last piece of the fish from the soup.

I drained the cup in silence.

At the end of the meal, Lu let me pay without making a show of grabbing for the bill. The waitress eyed us curiously, counting out the changes from a large plastic purse. A coin fell to the floor. Lu bent over to pick it up. The bangle around her bare ankle shone like from a dream.

I forgot to ask for his phone number as we parted outside Drunken South that afternoon. We were both slightly tipsy. I would come back, I believed. The store was only about ten minutes' walk away.

But I did not see him again during that trip, having to hurry back for a translation project in the States. There, shortly afterward, I started working on a novel set in China in the transitional period, about things happening in the country still so familiar yet at the same time so strange to me.

People say that the first book by an author cannot but bear autobiographical traces here and there. Well, if not with the main character, then with minor characters. The very beginning of the novels actually shows the protagonist preparing a dinner under the influence of his foodie friend nicknamed Overseas Chinese. In spite of initial hesitance, I kept Lu's surname as well as nickname, along with his characteristics.

Writing is sometimes capable of making one relive the past experience, and find new meaning in the process too.

The Song dynasty poet Su Dongpo compares one's life to the footsteps left by a solitary crane in the snow, with the traces visible for a moment, but soon gone. Trying to keep the footsteps there might be like the effort in the Sisyphus myth, but the effort made me go on writing.

It was more than three years later that I made the next trip back to China, carrying a copy of my first novel published in English. It had somehow turned into a mystery, but the character of Overseas

Chinese Lu changed little, except turning out to be more successful in fiction than in real life. I was looking forward to showing Lu the pages with his name in it, trying to imagine Lu's overjoyed response at our reunion.

"Oh the book is written by my friend in the United States. Look at my name in English."

> *Once more Lu declared that he had successfully started the business of his own--Moscow Suburb, a Russian-style restaurant on Huaihai Road, with caviar, pottage, and vodka on the menu, and a couple of Russian waitresses walking around in scanty dresses. Lu sounded so complacent and confident on the phone. It was beyond Chen to comprehend how Lu could have done everything at such short notice.*
>
> *"So business is not bad?"*
>
> *"It's booming, buddy. People come swarming in all day to look at our menu, at our vodka cabinet, and at our tall, buxom Russian girls in their see-through blouses and skirts."*
>
> *"You really have an eye for business."*
>
> *"Well, as Confucius said thousands of years ago, 'Beauty makes you hungry.'"*
>
> *"No. 'She is so beautiful that you can devour her,'" Chen said. "That's what Confucius said. How were you able to dig up these Russian girls?"*

> *"They just came to me. A friend of mine runs a network of international applicants. Nice girls..."*

For the trip, I checked into a hotel near Xizhuang Road. The next afternoon, I went to the delicatessen, thinking I might well buy a smoked carp head for the night snack if Lu happened not to be on the shift. To my surprise, in place of the delicatessen, I saw a newly-painted storefront selling fried chicken after the fashion of KFC, sporting an unmistakable American logo, which I had not seen in the States. Perhaps the location was too good for an old-fashioned Chinese delicatessen. In the midst of the economic reform sweeping over the country, a number of money-losing companies were bought over by others, as I had read in the States.

Lu was not there. One of the salesgirls busy arranging fried chicken legs and thighs in the glass counter looked familiar to me. I approached her.

"Lu's no longer here," she said simply, waving away a fly that circled the counter, insistently buzzing.

"But Duhongfang—"

"The delicatessen was sold. Now it's the American Chicken. I'm the only one left from the old days

"What about Lu?"

"He's at home on double guarantees."

"What does that mean?"

"It means he has lost his job, though the city government guarantees for his social security and medical insurance when he reaches retirement age."

"So he has no income now?"

"No, he has to eke out the best he can. But he's flying so high, you know. This small temple cannot house such a huge Buddha image. Now he is able to start his own grand business whatever way he likes," she said with sarcasm in her voice, killing the insistent fly with a determined swing of the plastic flap.

I was not too surprised at her reaction. It's just like Lu to talk in his expansive, exaggerated way. It had never really bothered me, but not so with my sister, nor with the salesgirl.

"Oh that—but do you have his home phone number or address?"

"No, I don't."

"What!"

I had taken it for granted that I could always get hold of him, one way or another. It was my fault.

Then I hurried back toward Baokang Lane, but to my utter dismay, the lane his sister had lived in also disappeared. There was nothing but a high rise in construction in the area.

According to my sister Xiaohong, the lane residents there had been relocated. She had heard nothing about the whereabouts of Lu's sister. I approached several former schoolmates. Only one of them said that he had seen Lu hawking hot tulip cakes in front of the delicatessen about two years earlier—possibly in a last ditch effort to save the business, but Lu turned his head in another direction. It struck me as understandable. It was by no means a job he would have been proud of. He avoided meeting his old schoolmates.

But even for such a face-losing job, eventually, he had failed to keep it.

I tried to recollect clues from our talk in the Drunken South, but the only possible one was about his apartment in Yangpu District. That's a too huge area. The white page did not help. He might not have had a phone at home.

At the end of the trip, I still had no luck. I left a copy of my book at home, asking Xiaohong to ask around for me, and to give it to Lu if she had any luck.

Back in the State, at the insistence of my American publisher, the stand-alone novel turned into a series, in which, Lu turns into a recurrent character, inviting Inspector Chen to be a partner for his fast-extended business, treating him lavishly, offering generous help, while continuing to open up new restaurants in the city of Shanghai. Soon an influential Big Buck in today's Shanghai. "*Number one in the Russian cuisine*" makes only one of the impressive titles in his business card.

> *[At Lu's insistence, Chen bring American poet Rosenthal to the new restaurant.] Moscow Suburb proved to be as splendid as Lu had promised. With its castle-like front, golden dome, and fully landscaped sides, Lu had totally transformed the appearance of the originally shabby restaurant, as if by magic. A tall blond Russian girl stood at the gate, greeting the customers, her slender waist supple like a young birch tree in a Russian folk song popular in the '60s.*
>
> *"Indeed, the current economic reforms are transforming China in a fundamental way," Rosenthal said.*

> *Chen nodded. Entrepreneurs like Lu were springing up "like bamboo shoots after a spring rain." One of the most popular slogans nowadays was "xiang qian kan." A play on Chinese pronunciation, in the '90s it now meant: " Look to the money!" The phrase had been a political slogan in the '70s, with the character "qian" written differently. Then, it meant "Look to the future!"*
>
> *With gorgeous Russian girls walking around in their miniskirts, the restaurant was doing a booming business. Every table was occupied. There were several foreigners dining there too.*
>
> *The Rosenthals and Chen were given a private room. The tablecloth gleamed snow white, glasses shimmered under highly polished chandeliers, and the heavy silverware could have been used by Czars in the Winter Palace...*

After all, Lu could have succeeded like that in the present-day China, and there seems to be some psychological comfort in contemplating his possible success in a society where material success is seen as the one and only success.

> *"Everything is possible in imagination in today's China," a young girl observes, nestling against Chen in the restaurant, licking a tender green tea leaf between her lips.*

To my surprise, a Chinese publisher contacted me for the possibility of having the novels translated back into Chinese. In spite of my initial misgiving about the censorship there, I agreed. That gave me another excuse to travel back and forth. In the midst of those trips, I kept asking about Lu. No news whatsoever, as if he had evaporated into the air. The American Fried Chicken had also disappeared, with the business sign outside changed at least three or four times.

Nevertheless, I found myself imagining, from time to time, of running across him around the street corner. It was unlikely in a large city like Shanghai, I knew. And I could not shake off the feeling that Lu in real life could have been drastically different from the one in the fiction, otherwise he would have contacted me.

With the release of the much-censored Chinese translation, I still had no luck finding Lu, except for a copy of *Three Musketeers* Xiaohong discovered for me at our old home. The very copy Lu had given me—with more vivid, colorful illustrations than all other editions I had since read.

And I left a Chinese copy of the Inspector novel at home, hoping Xiaolong would be able to give it to Lu.

"You have put Lu, but not me, into your novel. That's so unfair," Xiaohong mockingly complained.

"It's just because I have not heard anything about him for several years. With the Chinese translation out, he might happen to see his name in the book, so he could come to you."

"I don't think so. But Lu's just unlucky," Xiaohong said. "Old brand delicatessens like Duhongfang are staging a comeback in a collective nostalgia for the city. His was not that much of a job, but at least a state-run one."

Nodding, I was thinking of Lu from a different angle. In his younger days, Lu had tried so hard to go against the tide, but for how long could he have persevered? Eventually, he decided to move on like others, when the ever-changing time left him stranded on the shore. But it was understandable for Xiaohong to attribute it to his luck.

Ironically, the term "overseas Chinese" too was changing again in its connotation, at least not as such an enviable one like before. In this brave new world, the way Chinese upstarts showed off their wealth eclipsed the overseas Chinese. It's now fashionable for the latter to come back to China, looking for business opportunities. Hence a new term *"haigui"*—people who return from overseas to make money in China. Even western expatriates began talking about Chinese green cards in great gusto.

> *We calculate with our fingers / when the west wind will come, / unaware of time flowing away like a river in the dark...*

Early this year, I attended a comparative literature conference in Shanghai, giving my paper on the influence study. A tricky topic. One could have influenced another in ways never intended. Later, when the influenced tries to trace back to the source, it may prove to be totally irrelevant.

The afternoon the conference ended, I set out for a walk by myself, sauntering aimlessly for a while before I found myself heading toward the Bund. Drawing closer to the intersection of Yan'an and Zhongshan Roads, in the place of the once East Wind Restaurant, and then of KFC, I saw the newly renovated Waldorf Hotel, a magnificent new landmark of the city. Without stepping into it, I continued north along the water front. From the big clock atop the Custom House came wafting over a familiar melody, the same *East is Red* in eulogy of Mao. I cast a look toward the distant Bund Park with its gate embosomed in green leaves, and turned left to Nanjing Road, the present-day pedestrian street. I decided not to step into the Shanghai First Department Store, in which a character in the first Inspector Chen novel enacts the drama of her life and death in the early nineties. That afternoon, the building appeared shabby against the jostling new high rises around. Lost in thought, I arrived at Yan'an and Xizhuang Roads, where I climbed on the overpass, looking at the sun sinking in the west, obscured by the skyscrapers, before the realization hit home.

It was a route Lu and I had used to take in the seventies for our gourmet exploitation—except that there was no overpass at the time, nor so many new high rises around. Standing there, I looked down at the once delicatessen storefront beneath the overpass, and I thought of the lines by Li Bai:

> *"A cloud drifting, you keep / on traveling further, / further away. The sun setting, / I shall come here, long, / long thinking of you."*

Inspector Chen with Louis Vuitton in Longhua Temple

Chief Inspector Chen of the Shanghai Police Bureau was embarrassed to find himself the center of attention, returning the greetings from all around, and bowing to the incense-enveloped, black-framed pictures on the white wall of the Buddhist memorial service room, Longhua Temple.

He was there because of Peiqin, the wife of his long-time partner Detective Yu, who was having the service for her late parents. It was arranged in accordance to a popular belief that the deceased, upon reaching the age of one hundred, would move on to another world through reincarnation, and that the journey would most likely be smooth sailing with the monks chanting and sacrifices offering in a temple service. Peiqin had been such a loyal supporter to their work. Chief Inspector Chen could not say to her invitation.

As a rising Party cadre, Chen's presence for the occasion would have given a much-needed "face" to Peiqin and her relatives there, and in their imagination, to the deceased as well. The symbolism of the social status in today's China, that's all about it.

Withdrawing into a corner of the room, he observed several middle-aged women bending over in the opposite corner, busy folding the netherworld paper money into the shape of ancient silver and gold ingots, and putting them into the large dark brown trunks stacked up against the service table. On another similar occasion years earlier, Chen remembered, the ingots had been put into red paper bags. The imitation trunks, possibly made of cardboard sporting patterns vaguely familiar to him, looked impressively solid, high-end. The upgrade might have represented another "improvement with time," showing sophisticated consideration for the transportation in the other world.

Then the arrival of Lianping with a quick succession of the camera flashes in her hand broke the train of his thoughts. Young, gorgeous, she walked light-footed to him, and hugged him with a touch of exaggerated endearment, for the two of them had become known to each other for just about a week's time.

She was wearing a low-cut black dress, high heels, and a red-stringed *Wenhui Daily* name tag, apparently dressed for the occasion—for the man who appreciated her, as Confucius said thousands of years earlier. She lit a tall piece of incense and bowed together with him to the framed pictures on the service table. Her company at his side brought him back to the center of attention, stirring another wave of excited whispers through the room.

"Our celebrated Chief Inspector Chen wants me to come, so how can I possibly say no?" she said to Peiqin with a knowing smile. "I've been working on a profile of him for the newspaper, and the pictures here will come out with the article bearing the caption, 'Chief Inspector Chen kowtows with his partner at the temple—the genuine human side of a high-ranking Party official.'"

It was clever, considerate of her to have said all this for the benefit of the people attending the service. Chen wondered whether she would really put the pictures to use for the article. They had never discussed it. Still, the possibility of the pictures in the Party-run newspaper apparently meant a lot to the people there. He chose not to say anything about it.

In the midst of monks chanting the scripture, brass cymbals and wooden fish-shaped knockers beating in unison, he was required to kneel and kowtow at the ending of each section in the *Diamond Sutra*. Lianping held up the camera at him with a teasing smile.

Finally, with the service moving to its climax, Chen and Lianping walked out with others into the courtyard, following the file of chanting and singing monks. People gathered around a huge bronze burner and carried the silver-ingot-filled trunks into the flame. Chen noted the surprise flashing across her face as she raised her camera again, zooming in on the trunks.

"Louis Vuitton!"

Recognition hit home. The expensive world brand. That was how the trunks had stricken him as vaguely familiar inside. He had seen the brand in magazines and TV commercials.

"For an emerging Party official, and a celebrated modernist poet to boot, you may not need these brands or fake brands to sustain yourself." Lianping went on, reading the perplexity in his eyes, "But what about others? In a society with the materialistic success as the one and only criteria, how can people prove themselves as valuable? Haven't you heard of waves upon waves of shopping tourist groups swamping into Paris? 'Tourists' only in name, they simply snap Louis Vuitton, Hermes, Chanel and whatnot like locusts."

"But the imitation trunks here are burned in sacrifice!"

"Well, natural or supernatural projection. So the dead too could enjoy the top luxuries in the netherworld, if not in this world. Value added anyway."

She was perspective. Hadn't he found himself at the temple out of a similar consideration? To lend that valuable "chief inspectorship" of his to the occasion, so to speak. Perhaps for the same consideration, albeit subconsciously, he had asked Lianping to come to the service.

So here she was, a young attractive journalist of the Party newspaper in his company at the temple service, "adding more face" to his presence.

"After all, so many things are horrible fakes in today's China," she went on reflectively, "but this brand trunk may at least be evocative of a long acclaimed tradition, and of the reliable quality..."

In the midst of the entangled thoughts and associations, he was reminded of a real criminal case he had read about years earlier.

As early as the beginning of the last century, two criminals plotted to kidnap a successful publisher in Chicago by trussing him into a Louis Vuitton trunk, and carrying him out the hotel in secret. In their imagination, such a piece of luggage would make them look the least suspicious, but the publisher somehow escaped. Later on, one of the unlucky criminals hang himself in prison, and the pictures of the people involved as well as the trunk appeared in the newspaper...

Lianping's hand touched his as the flame started dancing over the trunks. In spite of her cynical interpretation, her touch was warm, soft, capable of bringing him back to the brave new world for the moment.

"A Louis Vuitton trunk filled with gold and silver ingots! It's really something to die for."

What might have happened to Chen Cao

Chief Inspector Chen of the Shanghai Police Bureau found himself waking out of a weird dream. Its details remained so vivid, and in a clear, convincing sequence that spanned many years, he could not help wondering who turned out to be real, the one moving up and down in the dream scenes, or the one lying on bed, breaking into a cold sweat.

He was momentarily disoriented, and reminded of the lines in a Tang dynasty poem by Li Shangyin. *"Waking in the morning, Master Zhuangzi wonders / whether he dreams of being a butterfly, / or a butterfly dreams of being Master Zhuangzi."*

Looking back, he found it even more unbelievable, ironically, that from a young man studying English in Bund Park, he had come all the way to his position as a Party-member police officer. Blinking in the morning light, and wiping the sweat from his forehead, he felt increasingly confused. There was one thing he knew, however. If he had just woken up from a dream, its details, while still vivid in mind, might begin to fade soon.

"What might have been and what has been / Point to one end, which is always present."

Those were the lines by T. S. Eliot, whom he liked.

And at present, he was practically drowning in political troubles. Though nominally still a chief inspector, he was barred from all the investigation work in the police bureau. He had no idea how long he could possibly survive, a chief inspector or not.

So he might as well put down the "dream scenes."

He then got up, ready for the work.

I (1971)

Chen was the youngest in the audience sitting at the evening talk in front of Red Dust Lane.

The contents of the evening talk changed with the time, of course. It was out of the question for people, in the middle of the Cultural Revolution, to say anything remotely "feudalist, bourgeois, and revisionist." The time-honored convention of the lane could have been banned, but for the intervention of Old Root, one of the most experienced narrators there, who managed to keep the evening talk alive by customer-tailoring it into a sort of political studies, waving a Little Red Book of *Quotations of Chairman Mao* in his hand. Being a worker in his class status, Old Root was capable of pulling a trick or two with impunity.

For instance, he made a point of choosing the stories mentioned favorably by Marx, Engels, Lenin, or Stalin as a sort of political endorsement, so Red Guards in the neighborhood had to think twice about finding fault with it. That evening, after declaring that Marx quoted from Dante's *Divine Comedy* in the front page of *Capital*, he recounted a romantic episode from the masterpiece.

"Marx could read Italian?" Chen asked.

"Of course he could. For *Capital*, Marx had to research in more than ten languages. 'Follow your own course and let others talk,' that's exactly what he quoted from Dante. And Marx said on another occasion, 'A foreign language is a useful weapon for your battle in life.'"

Afterwards, when most of the audience had left, Chen remained sitting on the bamboo stool, looking up to see the night clouds floating across the sky, aimlessly, like in a scroll of the traditional Chinese landscape.

He came to the evening talk because he had no idea about what to do with himself.

He had just graduated from Yaojin Middle School. It coincided with the onset of the national movement of "educated youths going to the countryside for reeducation from the poor and lower-middle class peasants." A political campaign launched by Mao to send millions of young people from the cities to the poor rural areas, where they were supposed to reform themselves through hard labor. Still, a small number of young people remained in the city with health problems, including Chen with the pretext of bronchitis. They were classified as "waiting-for-recovery youths," meaning they still had to leave the city, upon recovery, for the countryside.

Now, out of school, out of job, waiting with no light at the end of the tunnel, he worried himself sick. Later that evening, he had a talk with Yingchang, a neighbor in the lanes. Two or three years his senior, Yingchang was not counted as an "educated youth," having been assigned to a job in a state-run factory.

Yingchang suggested they go to Bund Park in the morning to practice tai chi, a popular exercise, and "politically okay" too. The park was not far from the lane. Chen jumped at the suggestion.

As it turned out, several others in the lane were also interested in the idea. The next morning saw a small group of them setting out for the park. Yingchang was eager to find an outlet for his young energy, which was being laid to waste in the dead-water-like factory. Sissy Huang joined simply because he followed Yingchang everywhere like a tail. Meili, an attractive woman in her early thirties, having recently divorced and turned in her immigration application to Hong Kong, had nothing else to do in Shanghai. Weiming, the eldest in the group, tagged along as another "waiting-for-recovery" youth.

As they were filing out of the lane, Chen heard several cocks crowing in succession. It was against the government policy to raise chickens in the city, but facing the severe shortage in food supply, those capable housewives managed to keep chickens out of sight—in the secret corners of their *shikumen* houses. After all, there were things far more important for the neighborhood committee cadres to worry about.

"Like in an old proverb, we practice sword to the cock's crow," Chen said, his steps quickening at recollection of an ancient legend. In the third century, a young hero practiced sword the moment a cock started crowing at dawn.

"Well, people play tai chi sword in the park too," Yingchang commented.

The park was an attraction in itself. In spite of its small size, the location made it popular to Shanghai people, its front gate facing the Peace Hotel across Zhongshan Road, and its back gate adjoining the Waibaidu Bridge, a name unchanged since its construction in the colonial era, meaning "*foreigners cross the bridge for free.*" At the Bund's northern end, the park opened to a curving promenade above the expanse of water joining the Huangpu and Suzhou Rivers, along with a panoramic view of vessels coming and going against the distant East China Sea.

In the school textbook, Chen had read that at the turn of the century, the park had been open only to Western expatriates with red-turbaned Sikh guards standing at the entrance, and with a large sign on the gate saying: *No Chinese or dogs allowed.* A true story or not, it was put into the history book for the sake of patriotism education, he guessed.

But he found it difficult to keep himself in high spirits, in spite of the ancient proverbs or the legend of the park.

Tai chi emphasized on moving slow rather than fast, subduing the hard by being the soft, in accordance to the Taoist yin-yang principle. In a small clearing called "tai chi square," he soon realized that tai chi did not become him. He was too young, too restless. While others made rapid progress, he stumbled, wrecking one pose after another. With him, "a white crane spreading out its wings" actually turned into "a white crane breaking its wings."

As for his Red Dust friends, they did not come to the park just for the sake of tai chi, either. Meili began to meet there with a married man nicknamed as "horse face," melancholy looking with a long face, carrying a Japanese camera with an unmistakable suggestion of being fashionable, and she posed for him with a Hong Kong umbrella twirling in the sunlight, leaning her upper body precariously over the water, her cheeks flushing, her smile blossoming into the flashing camera. Yingchang had his eye on a girl in a different tai chi group. Without having learned her name, he nicknamed her in secret as "graceful," in reference to her pose in *tuishou*, push-hand exercise, and practiced with her, palms to palms, pushing and being pushed in a slow, spontaneous flow, their bodies moving together in a seemingly effortless effort. The moment she became aware of his ulterior motive, however, she rotated her left forearm to ward off his advance, and he lost balance, staggering, and falling flat amidst people's laughter...

Chen saw no point his continuing to waste his mornings like that. Standing by the river, he recalled several lines in a Song dynasty ci poem, scanning the mist-mantled horizon in the distance, "*East flows the grand river, / the celebrated names rising and falling / through waves upon waves / for thousands of years...*"

Like in another Chinese proverb, there's no story without coincidence.

To the left of the "tai chi square," Chen saw a young girl sitting quietly on a green-painted bench, holding a book in her hand, her shoulder-length black hair occasionally rumpled by the breeze from the river. She read in absorption, paying little attention to the people moving around there. Behind her, the glistening dew drops clung to the verdant foliage, like a myriad of bright eyes waking up to the morning light in curiosity.

It was an uncommon scene. A popular political slogan those days declared that "It's useless to study," an ideological notion that underlay the movement of educated youths going to the countryside. Judging by the red plastic book cover, it would most likely be the *Selected Works of Mao* in her hand. However, she had on the bench a smaller book, which she also picked up from time to time.

Usually, she came around six, among the earliest regulars in the park, where she stayed until eleven. In all probability, a "waiting-for-recovery youth" too, out of school, out of work, just like Chen.

People could not help casting looks in her direction. Yingchang, too, came to walk around that bench, like a lone crow circling a night tree. According to his close-range observation, the smaller book was an English-Chinese dictionary, and the book in her hand was not the *Selected Works of Mao*, but an English textbook, for which she used the red plastic cover for camouflage. It was not too difficult to understand such a trick. Red-armbanded park patrollers could storm over any moment demanding: *For what purpose are you studying English in the Cultural Revolution?*

That posed no question to Chen, though. For the future, in which she believed.

And she appeared to be more than strikingly attractive, wearing a long red jacket, like blossoming against the verdant foliage around, her large, clear eyes looking up from the book, as if radiating with an inner beauty from within.

For him, she made the scene of the park.

If she could choose to study English for the future, what about him? He felt ashamed, of a sudden, about wasting his time like that.

But English books were not available in bookstores or libraries. He managed to get a set of the College English from his uncle, who had succeeded in transforming himself into an ordinary worker, with all the college textbooks stuffed and dusted in a cardboard box under the bed.

The next morning he came to the park with a first-year college English textbook, and chose an unpainted wooden bench not far from hers.

His change kept him away, however, from his tai chi friends, who came up with all sorts of interpretations for the abrupt shift. In their eyes, he must have fallen for the girl on the green bench, but instead of openly approaching her, he made just a pathetic attempt to catch her attention. Yingchang took the initiative on his behalf, which turned out not to be successful. Without giving out any details about it, Yingchang simply dubbed her as "Ice-and-Frost-Cold," a negative nickname that suggestive of her unapproachableness.

"That's not what I mean, Yingchang," Chen protested, "not at all,"

But that made him more nervous about approaching her. Whatever motivations attributable to his shift from tai chi to English, he just hoped that he would be able, one of those mornings, to speak to her in a language understandable only to themselves.

His mother became worried about his longer stay in the park, but his father, a high school teacher immersed in Taoism, calculated that it might prove to be propitious for the young man, elaborating on his favorite theory of five elements.

"For the name of our lane, Red Dust, there's too much soil, no water at all," his father said, concluding in terms of five elements. "But Bund Park, a place in close association with water, could be beneficial."

One mist-enveloped morning, sitting at his usual seat, he saw her glancing up from her books. Their eyes met for a second. She was wearing a pink sweater, silhouetted against the white clouds over the river. Aware of his gaze, she hang her head low with a shy smile, like a lotus flower swaying soft, supple, in a cool breeze—as in a short poem by Xu Zhimo. *"Softly, you hang your head low, / like a water lily, /shy, trembling in a cool breeze, / farewell, farewell, / with sweet sadness in your voice / SA YO U NA RA."*

Then he saw a stout, gray-haired old man shambling over to sit on the bench beside her. It was not something uncommon for people to share a bench in the park, but she seemed to start reading with the old man nodding aside, murmuring, and pointing at her open book, almost imperceptibly, when no one else was seen around.

So the old man was giving instruction to her English studies. Those days, English teaching in a public place could appear suspicious. Hence the deceptive appearance of the two— like two strangers who happened to sit on the same park bench.

Chen decided that, instead of approaching her, he too was going to consult the old man with questions in his studies.

The old man, surnamed Rong, was a retired English teacher. The outbreak of the Cultural Revolution cut short his teaching career, and he ended up coming to the park, offering help to the young people. He readily took Chen as another student.

Mr. Rong made a point, however, of talking with only one of his students at a time, wary of being seen as a teacher in the park. So there was no chance for the girl and Chen to sit together on the same green bench. But that was fine with Chen. No hurry for that. It took him less than two months to finish the first volume of the College English. Mr. Rong was impressed, spending more and more time with him.

The knowledge of her being there, with the book open on her lap, made it possible for him to progress by leaps and bounds, while marveling at the subtle change in her in the morning light. For one moment, a graceful blue stocking, nibbling at the top of a black fountain pen, but the next moment, a vivacious young Shanghai girl, curling her sandaled feet under her, a light green jade charm dangling on a thin string over her bosom. Behind her bench, a European-styled pavilion with its white verandah stood out in colorful relief.

One morning at the beginning of early September, to his surprise, she did not come to the green bench as usual.

He did not think too much of it, not initially. Unlike in school, people did not have to appear in the park every morning.

Then a week passed without seeing her stepping across the cobble trail to the green bench. What could have happened to her? There was hardly any way for him to find out.

He asked Mr. Rong, who did not know anything about it either. Not even her name or address. Perhaps somewhere close to the park, that was about all the old man could tell about her.

Once again, the group from Red Dust Lane was eager to offer interpretations about her evaporation in the air. Waving a cigarette like a magician's wand, Yingchang predicted that Chen would now come back to tai chi.

But Chen went on with his English studies, glancing up from the book, from time to time, at the unoccupied green bench.

Weeks, and months passed. The river flowed on, with white gulls hovering above the waves, their wings flashing against the gray light, as if soaring out of a half-forgotten dream. More than once, he did not leave the park until the dividing line between the Huangpu and Suzhou Rivers became invisible in the gathering dusk.

One day she would come back, he believed, to find him still sitting there, on the bench close to hers. They would then speak to each other in English.

The members of the Red Dust group began to drop out, one by one, like the leaves with the arrival of the autumn wind. None of them turned into a martial arts master.

Chen was the only one left in the park, where he started studying the third volume of the College English. Mr. Rong, too, appeared less in the park because of his high blood pressure, but Chen managed to continue studying by himself.

One afternoon, he mounted a flight of the stone steps to the bank. To his right, he saw a white-haired man practicing tai chi in leisure, wearing a white silk martial arts costume, loose-sleeved, red-silk-buttoned, moving in perfect harmony with the *qi* of the universe, striking a series of poses, the names of which Chen still remembered: *grasping a bird's tail, spreading a white crane's wings, strumming the pipa lute, parting a wild horse's mane on both sides...*

Would he have turned into such a master had he persisted in practicing tai chi? He wondered, breathing in the familiar tangy air from the waterfront.

Standing there, he reopened the book in his hand. It was an English novel titled *Random Harvest*, in which there were quite a number of words he did not really understand, but he managed to follow the storyline. It had been made into a movie, he heard, with a romantic title in the Chinese version: *Reunion of Mandarin Ducks*. The water birds were symbolic of lovers in classical Chinese culture.

A fitful wind was tearing at the page. It was not a spot for him to read. He closed the book. Looking over his shoulder, he suddenly saw her again—still in the pink sweater, sitting on the same bench, the bush behind trembling eerily in a breeze—

Half way down the steps, he acknowledged it to himself that it was another young girl, carrying a genuine Little Red Book in her hand.

The morning's in the arms of Bund, her hair dew-sparkled...

He was thinking about the ending of the English novel, in which Paula ran over the hills toward Smith, praying that the miracle could be real.

II (1988)

It was an early spring evening. Chen had just finished a meeting in the Peace Hotel, which now opened to Chinese as well as Western customers in the late eighties.

He stepped out and headed to Bund Park. It was close. Sometimes, he thought better while walking. Particularly along the river. It could be a crucial decision for him.

He slowed down at the sight of a swarthy sailor coiling the hawsers with cruise passengers waiting in the dark, the current somber, and the bell urgent.

The Bund appeared vibrantly alive that evening, with lovers sitting on concrete benches, nesting in the patches shades, standing along by the bank. The river, though still polluted, exhibited signs of improvement. Across the expanse of water shimmering with neon lights, the Pudong area presented new impressive buildings scattering out in the erstwhile farmland.

He walked in through the iron-wrought park gate, across a small square toward a green-painted bench under a tall poplar tree. It had been his usual seat. On the back of the bench was a slogan carved in the late sixties: Long *Live the Proletarian Dictatorship*! The bench must have been repainted several times, but the engraved message showed through the lapse of time.

Like everything else in the city, the park, too, had been changing. So had Chen himself— from a "waiting-for-recovery youth" to a young emerging scholar.

He did not take his seat. On a cool April breeze, a melody came over from the big clock atop the Shanghai Customs Building.

Different from the one during the Cultural Revolution: "The East Is Red."

Time flowed like water.

Chen had just received two extraordinary offers.

One of them came up in the hotel. It was for him to serve as an editor in chief for a series of cultural studies—*Marching toward the New Century*. He did not have to work like a full-time editor in a publishing house. His responsibilities consisted of selecting the topics, studying the proposals, and making decisions. He could still teach at the university.

The other offer was a prestigious fellowship as a visiting scholar to the United States. He could pick up a university there to further his research. But that meant he had to be away from China for at least one year, and such a prospect that would rule out his taking charge of the series.

Taking a breath in the familiar twang from the river, he found himself more inclined to the fellowship. It would be a good opportunity for him to continue his studies. As for the editing of the series, there're too many uncertainties involved.

He began strolling along the bank, letting his mind play back fragments of the discussion in the hotel.

"These books will exercise the influence, not only for this century," Ruan, the editor of Shanghai Publishing House, said in the shadow of an antique lamp in the hotel cafe, "but for the next century too. That's why we call it 'March toward the New Century.' China is at a crossroad right now, you know. A well-known poet as well as a critically-acclaimed scholar in comparative literature and culture, you are the very man for the job, Profess Chen."

In the late eighties, for all the momentum gained in China's economic reform, the political reform remained as an empty promise in the Party newspapers. Consequently, some young intellectuals believed they had to deal with the problems at the root of the culture, and others wanted to introduce the latest western thoughts. A series of literary, cultural, social, philosophical studies might serve to meet the need, but Chen chose not to make any commitment in the hotel.

"In a time like this," Ruan concluded, "we have to think about things larger than ourselves, Professor Chen."

A siren was sweeping over from the river. Chen headed out of the park. The reflection of neon lights kept flashing over the waves multicolored messages in Chinese and English. To his left, Zhongshan Road stretched on, a long vista of magnificent buildings, which had once housed those Western companies in the early part of the century, and then the Communist Party institutions after the fifties, now welcoming back the Western companies. It was said to be an effort to enhance the Bund's status in the world.

He nearly bumped against a young girl hurrying over like a moth fluttering, blindly, toward the entrance of the park where a young man was waving his hand. She was wearing a long red jacket, almost like a trench coat. Chen was vaguely reminded of someone he had seen years earlier, but like in a Tang dynasty line, "Only it was getting elusive, even there and then."

Shaking his head, he tried to dispel the confusing thoughts. He had to concentrate on the decision. For the series, he might well include a book by himself on the history of the park, highlighting its change in the colonial and post-colonial backgrounds, and in the Cultural Revolution too. New historicist studies sometimes start with concrete anecdotes—for his book, a vignette of his English studies in the park, possibly including the mysterious disappearance of the girl on the green bench. Exhilaration quickened his steps.

Absentmindedly, he turned north, crossed the bridge, and moved on. The night breeze was refreshing. No hurry to go back to the attic room in Red Dust Lane.

He then found himself getting lost in a maze of winding streets, one of them still covered in cobble stone. It was somewhere in Hongkou district. He wandered on, the moon overhead hiding momentarily behind the night cloud. It took longer than he expected to reorient himself. A night bird was flushed up at his footsteps. It was a quiet night. A poem by Su Dongpo came back to mind.

"*The waning moon hangs on the sparse tung twigs, / the night deep, silent. / An apparition of a solitary wild goose / moves like a hermit. // Startled, it turns back, / its sadness unknown to others. / Trying each of the chilly boughs, / it chooses not to perch. / Freezing, the maple leaves fall / over the Wu River.*"

Su wrote the piece in exile, supposedly about the choice he had to make in his political career, but Chen was not too sure about it.

It was beginning to drizzle when he caught sight of a small restaurant tucked in at a street corner, with a white wooden sign beneath a red lantern: "Small Family." Perhaps one of the private-run restaurants—something new in the city in the middle of China's economic reform.

He stepped into the restaurant which, presumably converted out of a residential room attached with a courtyard in an original *shikumen* house, was cozy and comfortable, though with only four or five rough wooden tables inside. A hansom woman was sitting at the other end of the room, reading a magazine in the soft light at a makeshift counter.

She rose upon his entrance, walked over, and led him to a table by the window looking out to a row of flower pots in the courtyard.

Apparently, she was the owner, the waitress, and possibly the chef—all in one, plus a hostess at home too, wearing soft-heeled slippers, and a white apron embroidered with pink apricot blossoms. He took a quick look at the menu she handed him. An interesting variety of home style specials of the city, including cold dishes like tofu in sesame oil, dices of thousand year egg, half of the smoked carp head. Inexpensive, yet possibly delicious.

"There's no knowing which direction the wind is blowing...no knowing..." fragments of a popular song came wafting over from a cassette player somewhere behind the counter. The lines seemed to be based on a poem by Xu Zhimo, a romantic modernist poet Chen liked.

"I'm not that hungry," he said. "A couple of small dishes will do. And a cup of beer."

"Yes, it's late," she said with an engaging smile. "To start with, I would recommend chicken immersed in rice wine, and cold tofu mixed with green onion and sesame oil. Qingdao beer."

What she recommended appeared not to be the expensive ones on the menu. He nodded his approval.

"How about the across-the-bridge noodles afterward? We'll serve the chicken first for the beer, and then use the remaining portion for the noodles."

"That's intriguing." He remembered having heard about the origin of "across the bridge noodles," a folk story of a capable wife managing to serve the noodles hot, fresh across the bridge to her hard-studying husband.

A true story or not, it was a sort of service showing consideration for the customer, which he had not enjoyed in state-run restaurants.

It was because, he thought, she worked for her own business, rather than for the state-owned.

He nodded again before taking out the notebook, trying to go over the points scribbled down earlier in the hotel. It was not going to be an easy job for him to take over the series, he began to think more soberly. Some of the topics could be controversial. As its editor, he might have to bear the brunt. So far, the authorities had been fairly tolerant of him, but the political weather could change overnight. He had to walk the tight rope all the time. But then his thought shifted to the project about Bund Park. Possibly an original one—not just for himself. He produced out of his briefcase an English book on Shanghai history.

Dishes appeared on the table. She remained standing aside as if waiting for his approval, her hands crossed in front of the dainty apron.

He raised the chopsticks. The chicken tasted tender, rich with the rice wine aroma. The cold tofu flavored with green onion and sesame oil was delicious too. Both of the dishes proved to be up to the multi-requirements of color, smell, and taste for a self-claimed gourmet like him. The beer fresh and cold. Almost perfect for an early spring evening. He nodded again.

Her face lit with a shy smile, she went back to her reading behind the counter.

Sipping at the beer, he caught his mind wandering away, unexpectedly, to a short story by Yu Dafu, which was titled "The Evening Intoxicated with the Spring Breeze."

It was perhaps because of the family atmosphere, not just because of the dishes.

After connecting the points in the notebook with lines and adding some words in the margin, he thought he had a better grasp of the decision waiting for him. He took another sip and saw her moving to his table again, carrying a small bowl of grape.

"It's on the house," she said. "Desert after you have finished the noodles."

"An excellent meal," he said. "The business must be good during the day."

"Not bad. Thank Buddha. We have some real specials here. For instance, the spicy fish head pot. The live fish all the way from the Thousand Island Lake. A lot of customers come back for it. But you already have ordered your noodles tonight."

She cast a look at the English book on the table, hanging her head low, smiling again, like a water lily slightly shy in a cool breeze—

Recognition came—fragmented at first, like waking up in a morning haze—the way the girl on the green bench reacted when she first became aware of his attention.

He remembered it. It was her, the girl studying English in Bund Park, who had since turned into an infallible source of inspiration. For him, the subsequent changes came—albeit indirectly—all through this first link in the long, long chain.

Thanks to her, those dew-decked mornings in the park sustained him through the years of the Cultural Revolution, and then to the highest score on English in the college entrance examination in 1977. After four years, it was also because of his English score he was admitted as a MA student for comparative literature, and upon graduation offered a position at the university.

His glance fell in confusion, to her bare feet in the slippers, her red-painted toes flashing like fallen petals.

"No one is a tree, / standing entire of itself. / The wind that breaks the petal / also breaks me."

After so many years, however, he could not be so sure that it was she, not just because of the way she hang her head low with shy smile.

"Excuse me," he said, looking up. "I think I may have seen you—years ago."

"Really?"

"Did you study English at Bund Park in the early seventies?"

"Yes, I happened to be there—for fun—for a couple of months."

"Remember a young man who also studied English there—sitting at a bench not far from yours?"

"A young man who also studied English there—" she sounded dubious, eying him up and down.

It was understandable that she did not remember him the way he remembered her, he hastened to tell himself.

"There, I think, but—so you're the one?"

"Yes, that's me. I took you as my role model there," he said. "Thanks to those days in the park, I passed the college entrance examination with the highest score in English in 1977. Now I'm teaching at Shanghai University."

"Congratulations!"

"I was, and I still am, so grateful to you. I looked for you in the college years." It was true that he had made several attempts to find her, and in other colleges too, believing that she must have been studying as a college student like him, but without success. "Little did I think I would meet you this evening! Oh, how are things with you?"

"Not too bad. We started earlier than others, so we have quite a number of regulars here. And hopefully we're going to expand soon."

She sounded vague, perhaps in reference to her restaurant business only.

He found himself at a momentary loss for what else to say. A short spell of silence engulfed the room. She remained standing there, her black hair held back by a dark blue cotton scarf, her face slightly pale in the light.

After all, they had started on the same beginning line, so to speak, but what now? She was a *getihu*—"individual business licensee," a term hardly positive, if not too negative, in China's socialist system. In the newspapers, it was discussed as a sort of not-that-legitimate supplement to the central-government-planned economy.

Was she going to spend her life like this—cooking and serving, day in and day out, wiping all the imagination away on her apron in the eatery? He failed to connect her with the girl studying in the park.

And he recalled something said by Yingchang, a tai chi companion in the park those days, "She's really special to you."

Chen had never admitted so to himself. At that moment, however, he was no longer too sure about it. Why would he have been so shocked by the change in her?

In existentialism, one may be said as no more than the sum total of his or her choices, but one is not always able to choose freely—not in China. Would it be fair for him to hold her responsible for the choices and then, the consequences?

He did not have an answer to this.

There must have been a long story about her journey from the park to the restaurant. Was she going to tell him that? He recalled a Witgensteinian paradigm: *What we cannot speak about must pass over in silence.*

But there was a question which, if not answered, could haunt him afterward, he knew. Did his appearance in the park, no matter how inadvertently, cause her disappearance? In the lambent light of the restaurant, the question was getting more urgent for him.

He had often thought of it, conjuring up a variety of interpretations. She could have been bothered by his presence—the implied advance from an unknown young man, purposely sitting nearby and holding an English book in hand. In another scenario, was it because the old teacher Rong spent more and more time with him, rather than with her?

He pulled out a chair for her. The two seated themselves at the table, sitting closer than in the park, facing each other.

Instead of raising the question, he shifted to the story of how she had been inspiring him through these years.

She listened to his narrative without making any interruption, except to rise to add hot water into his cup. It was quieter in the room. She leaned slightly forward at the table, her slender fingers touching the greenish grapes, squeezing and breaking a tiny one in spite of herself.

The narrative could have sounded ironical to her, he realized. After all, what had happened to the one who had inspired him in the days at the park and afterward?

In the ensuing silence, he heard a faint sound in the back.

"My husband snores," she said with a suggestion of embarrassment. "He and our son Qiangqiang sleep in the back."

It was as he had suspected. A family restaurant—with the family living behind the restaurant business area. It was none of his business, though.

Then it was her turn to tell him about what had happened to her.

Like him, she was a "waiting-for-recovery youth" in the early seventies. It was out of boredom that she went to the park, where she happened to see an old man reading a *Quotation of Chairman Mao* in English. Curious, she asked him questions about it, and he offered to help. So she started studying there.

It was not easy, however, for a young girl to do so. One of her neighbors saw her holding a book there, reading, sitting beside a man. Gossips and speculations began surfacing in her neighborhood. Her worried parents had a talk with her. She had imagined that English would be useful one day, but "one day" appeared to be a too remote possibility, for which she did not want to fight with her parents. She tried to continue her studies at home, but what with all the distractions imaginable in one single small room, and then with all the housework for her when her mother suffered a stroke, she gave up.

After the Cultural Revolution, she did not take the college entrance examination. She worked at a neighborhood workshop, and married a co-worker there. In the early eighties, her husband was disabled with a severe work injury. She, too, quit her job to help him run the small family restaurant.

So it went all the way to the present—just like that.

She spoke in a subdued voice, probably because of her family sleeping behind the partition wall, he supposed.

It was not much of a story. Also, he was disappointed because of his absence in it. Still, the "speculations" about her in the park, though far from detailed, could have involved him—with him sitting nearby, and holding a book too. More likely for a young man than an old one to prop up as a suspect in people's imagination. But he chose to say nothing.

In retrospect, life seemed to be so full of the *ironical causalities of misplaced Yin and Yang*, like the misplaced interest in tai chi, the misplaced imagination on the green bench, the misplaced speculation... One thing led to another, to still another, and the result could hardly be recognized.

Would it be better had they not met again this evening?

"Oh, it's late," he said abruptly.

"Don't worry. It'll stay open till twelve, and you have not had your noodles—"

But it was already past twelve. The tofu, no longer fresh-looking, appeared a bit watery in the dish. Half of the chicken remained untouched. He did not want to wait for the cross-bridge noodles.

"I'm afraid I have to leave. It's so nice to meet you again," he said. "Let me know if there's anything I can do for help."

That sounded so hypocritically empty, even to himself. What help possibly from him to her for the restaurant business?

She walked with him to the door in her soft-heeled slippers. It was wet, dark outside with only one street lamp gleaming on. A violin melody came rippling over, intermittently, from a window above the curve of the deserted street.

He said goodbye to her, and handed her a business card of his.

"Keep in touch."

He turned to walk away, but he looked back over his shoulder after half a dozen steps. He failed to catch another glimpse of her retreating into the light of the Small Home. He stood still, fumbling for a cigarette in his pant pocket.

He was about to resume walking when he heard steps approaching him from behind.

She caught up with a notebook in her hand—the one he had left behind on the table. "It's yours, Chen. You were writing on it."

"Thanks. It's about a project I may not--" he did not finish the sentence, aware of the light glistening in her clear eyes.

"When I looked at your card," she said in a hurry, grasping the notebook. "I remembered having seen you on TV. You're doing something important today. Please go on —not just for yourself, but for others not as lucky as you."

He was surprised at her comment, which seemed to be touching a chord deep in him--still resounding, after these years.

"Yes, I think I'm going to make up my mind—after tonight's—"

So he was going to choose the project of *Marching toward the New Century*. He was lucky—because of her. And he owed all that to her, the idealistic dreams instilled in him in Bund Park. It's least he could do to send her a set of the books upon the completion of the series. She would understand.

There is a meaning, perhaps, in the loss of the meaning.

It was then he heard anther siren coming over from the river, reverberating, and then fading in the dark.

III (2008)

She woke up with the broken images of a dream lingering in the back of her mind. The fragments were disconnected, yet singularly disconcerting.

Alone, she is climbing a wrought-iron staircase to a large cedar deck jutting out on the Bund, overlooking the moonlight-flecked water. The night still young, lovers lined along the bank, like snails stuck in a row against the embankment, they were nestling or whispering to each other in intimacy, regardless of others standing next to them, and of a red-armbanded patrollers stalking around. Leaning against the railing, she finds herself listening to the waves lapping against the shore, clutching an apple in her hand. Gulls hovering over from the darksome vessels in a distance, she shifts her glance to a somber-colored sampan swaying in the tide under her gaze. A wave shovels at the sampan, bringing down a cloth diaper from a clothesline stretched across the deck.

"A family sampan with the couple working down in the cabin," she hears herself murmuring to a tall man beside, chewing a piece of gum, and blowing out a bubble in the lambent moonlight, "and living there too, day and night."

"A torn sail married to a broken oar," he responds readily, like out of a poem.

As if in cue to their talk, a chubby baby starts crawling out of the cabin under the discolored tarpaulin, looking up to them, and grinning like a Wuxi earthen doll.

She lets him take up her hand and throws the apple down to the baby in the boat. Of a sudden, they seem to have the river to themselves.

"*Not the river, but the moment / it starts rippling in your clear eyes...*" he says to her. The big clock atop the Custom Building begins chiming, and sending the melody of East Is Red through the night breeze—

But it turned out to be the phone shrilling on the nightstand. She was reaching out her hand when the ringing stopped.

She looked at the watch. Almost one thirty in the afternoon. The sunlight was streaming through the large window. For all the world, she could not figure out the identity of the man in the dream scene, speaking at her side like reading a love poem.

When a young girl, she, too, had loved poetry, but it was so long ago, almost in another life. In the dream, she must have been only seventeen or eighteen, judging from the surrounding scenes—still characteristic of the early Cultural Revolution, during which period she often went to Bund, particularly to the park for a short while, she remembered.

Who was he? Surely not her late husband, who was by no means a man of letters. Besides, she had not even met him those days.

An inexplicable sense of anxiety gripped her, and of inconsolable loss too, as if being transported back to the days when she was as poor as the ones in the sampan.

A siren came from the river. She got out of bed, drawing aside the curtain. Looking at her reflection in the window, she felt a slight chill on her bare arms in spite of the sunlight. She still had a hangover from a late business party last night, with a group of Big Bucks toasting to the success of her "Shanghai Number One" real estate company. Indeed, she had moved so far, far away from the girl in the dream. No way of her turning back to that young, naïve one standing on the Bund, clutching an apple.

But the phone rang again, breaking into her thoughts.

"Good news about the Red Dust Lane project, Xia."

"Oh, Ouyang. It's just like you—with the first word in the morning about business."

"Still in the morning, Xia?" Ouyang chuckled. "I've talked to Old Zhou, the guy in charge of the city development. Because of its city center location, it's an unbearable eyesore. And even more so for the coming World Expo in 2010. The old shabby lane absolutely has to disappear from the city map."

"People have talked about it for a long time," she said. "There must be a reason for their having not yet done so."

But she knew why. Because of the risks involved. In the past, a developer could have easily relocated the residents with something of a government document plus a symbolic sum of compensation. With the housing price continuing to soar, however, people began to know only too well about the potential worth of their property. So they stuck on, like nails unyielding to the pressure of the official demand and not-so-official violent demolition. With the current emphasis on a harmonious society, any protest or fight breaking out in the demolition could turn into a political disaster for the developers, and for the officials behind them too.

"This time, it's totally different—the city image for the World Expo," he responded. "Also, there will be a new subway cutting across there, with the station located close to the site of the lane. The area around will be classified as the priority of the city development."

So it was the old trick, yet under the new name— the World Expo. People might not be able to resist or negotiate.

"Whatever excuse or reason, some people won't believe it, not after so many development scandals."

"But we have to push ahead, Xia. Time and tide wait for no man."

"I'm a woman, Ouyang," she said.

What he said, however, was true. In a new expression in the Chinese language, to run business is to *jump into the sea*, which spells risks as well as opportunities. She had started from a small family restaurant, but thanks to one of unbelievable opportunities, which came in her serving a steaming hot bowl of wanton soup on a cold, rainy evening to Ouyang, then a district production group director, and his taking a fancy to her soup—to be more exact—to her placing the soup on the table, hanging her head low with a shy smile that "flashed up the gray wall." ...

He had since enjoyed a rocket rise in his career, all the way to his present position as the assistant to the Mayor of the city. And she too had moved along in his company, sailing to her multi-billion yuan success like in a dream.

"For this project, a lot of people's interests are at stake—some of them high above us. With the old lane remaining on that corner, the property value for the whole area will never rise," he concluded on the phone. "You don't have to worry. When the sky falls, it's up to those above to shoulder it up."

It was a discussion longer than expected. When she put down the phone, the clock's hand was drawing toward two thirty.

There was nothing important in the company that afternoon, she checked, and made herself a cup of coffee.

Perhaps it would not be a bad idea for her to go and take a look at Red Dust Lane. To further explore the feasibility of the project. Ouyang might not a reliable narrator with his own business interest involved—as an undisclosed partner of the Shanghai Number One Real Estate Company.

The maid knocked before moving in, put a bowl of swallow nest on the table, and said respectfully, "It's still warm, Madam. You were talking on the phone, so I kept the bowl in hot water."

Xia did not like swallow nest, but she helped herself to one spoonful. A Fujian business associate had sent her a large box of it, so expensive with its supposed enhancement to a woman's youthful look. The local farmers had to collect the wild nests on the steep cliffs, and it would be too much of a waste for her not to finish it.

After taking a quick shower, she dressed herself in a light gray short-sleeved cashmere suit and walked out.

The car was already waiting on the driveway. The chauffer Big Zhang hurried out to open the door for her. "Where, Madam?"

"Red Dust Lane," she said. "On the corner of Fujian and Jinling Roads."

"You are visiting a friend there?" Big Zhang said. "It's like a forgotten corner of the city."

It probably came from a movie title, "A Corner Forgotten by Love," which she had seen in the early eighties, about young people struggling in a poor village.

"Yes, for someone there I have not seen for years," she said vaguely. No point revealing the real purpose of the visit. Speculations could start easily these days.

She seated herself in the back of the car, took out a small mirror, and noted some fine lines—"fish's tails" as described in a Tang dynasty poem, she still remembered —around the corners of her eyes.

Time swims away, like in the water, like in a dream.

For her, perhaps not a bad dream, as part of a larger, more dramatic saga—the incredible, dream-like rise of China. In the early summer of 2008, its success story was reaching another climax, with the Olympic going to take place in Beijing, and then in another two years, with the World Expo coming in Shanghai.

But there's no secret for her business success. All because of the land, which belonged to the state, i.e., to the Party cadres in the position to sell it—in the name of the economic reform—to one developer or another through their connections. In her case, thanks to Ouyang's government position and connection, with his invaluable help from the beginning. With an extraordinarily large compensation for the "premium business property" of her restaurant when pulled down for city development, she was able to purchase the land nearby with the inside information from him, at the inside price too, not to mention a number of bank loans arranged by him. It was also through his business planning that she started up a real estate company, which soon expanded by leaps and bounds.

After the untimely death of her husband, Ouyang came to her place more often than before, and that as a business partner too, as Shanghai ushered in an unprecedented boom of housing construction.

Several projects under her were ballooning to more than a hundred thousand yuan a square foot...

The vibration of her cell phone broke into her reveries. Again, the LCD showed Ouyang's name. She did not want to discuss with him in the car, however, about her visit to the lane.

For the last two or three years, he did not come to see her that much. A sort of distance between them would be prudent, particularly with her son Qiangqiang becoming a college student. Also, Ouyang had had his share of "little secretaries," younger and prettier, she knew. She was not really upset about it, but there were other things she had heard about him, which sometimes sent a chill down her spine.

"The city traffic is impossible," Big Zhang said, shaking his head like a rattle drum, "with at least three hundred new cars coming to the road every day."

"Take your time, Big Zhang. It's not for any business meeting today."

It took more than one hour for them to reach the lane, which came in view like a shabby, solitary isle surrounded by seas of high rises.

She told Big Zhang to drive around the area for a couple of times before pulling up near the back entrance of the lane. It was close to a large food market she had heard of, where she was surprised to see only a few stalls scattered here and there, far less than she had imagined.

"You go back home first, Big Zhang," she said, stepping out of the car. "I don't know how long I'll stay here. Qiangqiang may need you."

She started walking toward the lane, looking up to its name inscribed on the stone arch of the back entrance: **Red Dust Lane**. Two or three bats were seen hovering around the arch in an eccentric flurry.

Immediately, she became aware of the glances from several youngsters lounging at the entrance, smoking, cursing, and shouting loudly as if they were the only people that mattered in the world.

"*Go forward bravely, young girl*," one of them started singing in a strident voice, obviously in reference to her—an incongruous figure heading diffidently for the lane, though she was not young any more.

Against the surrounding skyscrapers, the lane represented a sharp contrast, dirty, sordid, revealing its helpless tears and wears through the years. Overhead, the dripping clothing along the bamboo poles across the lane nearly obliterated the sky. Not too many people here had washing machines at home, she could tell. The laundry also spoke about the large number of the residents in the lane, which concerned the relocation expense of the prospective project.

Not to her surprise, she saw a wooden chamber pot airing outside in the declining light. A wet bamboo broom stood leaning against the bare wall, like an inverted exclamation mark against the black-pained door of the *shikumen* house. A drop of water fell down on her cheek. An ominous sign, she thought frowning, but she was hit with a sense of de javu, though pretty sure that she had never stepped into the lane before. Several middle-aged or elderly people looked in her direction. There were sitting or standing out of their homes, one holding a large bowl of rice, another stretching on a ramshackle bamboo recliner, and still another scaling a belt fish vigorously in a moss-covered common sink.

Nevertheless, she felt drawn toward the scenes of the lane, which struck her as intimate, as if with someone familiar waiting for her there. Apparently, the neighbors in the lane still enjoyed close relationship and interactivities, though necessitated, ironically, by the cramped space. She herself had grown up in such a neighborhood. But Shanghai was becoming more and more like other metropolitans in the world—New York, London, Paris, with towering high rises and mega shopping malls, yet practically identical from one to another. Probably the same could be said about those internationally famous brands there—nothing but conspicuous consumption. And she cast a self-conscious glance at the LV purse in her hand.

It took her only about two minutes to move through the lane, to the front entrance, where she noticed an antique-like blackboard, presumably black-painted-and-repainted, botched with the latest painting peeling. It turned out to be a blackboard newsletter written in chalk. The concept of such a newsletter, too, was out of time. She wondered how many people would still read it today.

Coming out onto Jinling Road, she saw a small group of people sitting out in front of the lane, mostly white-or-gray-haired ones, some of them in shorts, stripped to the waists, and some of them, in threadbare pajamas. In the middle of them, an elderly man was talking, and others were listening attentively.

To the left of the group, there was a middle-aged man sitting by himself on a bamboo stool, beside a dark wooden chair, over which was draped a paper scroll that declared in bold brush strokes: *Tell your fortune through a character you choose for yourself.* Apparently, a fortune teller who practiced by reading the characters, he was wearing a "culture shirt" with printed Chinese characters—a fashion popular among foreign tourists—which nonetheless carried a halo of authenticity.

It was a practice of Chinese glyphomancy, which she had seen in a Beijing opera entitled *Fifteen Strings of Copper Coins*. In the opera, a disguised judge tricked a full confession out of a murderer by performing such a character divination. It works because a Chinese character can have multifarious meanings in itself, as well as in its combination with other characters. In addition, a character is capable of breaking down into meaningful radicals or common component parts, so the possibility of its interpretations is unlimited.

She had never believed in fortune telling. But that late afternoon, she slowed down her steps, conscious of an incomprehensible premonition. Was it because of the prospective real estate project? Anyway, it would not hurt for her to have a talk with him, who might tell her something, if nothing else, about the neighborhood.

"Hi, Madam, my mundane surname is Chen, a poor scriber in the world of red dust," the fortune teller started before she could have uttered a word. "While it is but a humble profession, it takes a lot of training to give accurate interpretation. I won't misread or misguide my customer for anything. You may rest assured about that."

"Can you really read such a lot from one single character?"

"Everything comes and goes in illusion, of which our whole world is made up," he said. "Interpretation helps to make sense of it."

"It sounds too abstract to me."

"Well, it's like you're looking for the ox while riding on its very back. Eventually, you may find the answer right in your own heart. My practice simply helps to make it easier."

It sounded like paraphrasing of a Zen paradox, but she was in no mood for any metaphysical discussion.

"With so much unknowable in today's world, a 'divine interpretation' may be as good as any other help. Yes, I think I could use one."

"You really have a wisdom root, Madam. When Cangxie first created the system of Chinese language, every archetypal stroke came out of the cosmos in correspondence to the omnipresent qi, and in turn, in correspondence to the micro-cosmos of an individual human being. Indeed, *tianren heyi*—heaven-and-human in one. Whatever character you may choose to write, there will be elements recognizable from the mysterious correspondence."

"What about two people writing the same character?"

"Well, illusion rises from your own heart. What can be everything to one may be nothing to another. A good or a bad world really depends on the deepest thoughts, conscious or unconscious, in your mind. So go ahead and choose a character. If you find my interpretation neither here nor there, you may walk away without having to pay me a single penny. " He closed his eyes, deep-breathing like in meditation, before handing her a brush pen. "Fortune or misfortune is self-sought. Human proposes, Heaven disposes. Now please write a character arising from your heart."

She did not consider herself easily gullible to such ambiguous mumbo-jumbo. But there was something about the man opposite her. Suddenly she was not so sure.

"*Ao--*" she murmured, debating with herself whether to play along.

"*Ao* as the first character in Olympic in Chinese?"

135

So she wrote the character ao on the paper, though it had just been an exclamation on her part. Still, one character could be as good as another.

"Is that related to Olympic?"

"No," she said. "Not exactly."

It was related, however, in an ironic way. One of the contributing factors for the China's housing market fever was that of the Olympic. The property price began shooting up like a rocket the day it was announced that Beijing would serve as the sponsor for the Olympic.

"Well, things as small as a bird's pecking or sipping, are all related or interrelated under the sun," he said, producing those phrases like beer bubbles. "An interesting character--*ao* also as in *aomiao*—mysterious and miraculous. About something unknown to you, and you want to find more about it, right?"

"Well—" *Aomiao*, which is *ao* in combination with miao. That was not what she meant. But then what could she say about these mysterious, if not that miraculous, changes in her life?

"While the character seems to be positive in its general connotation, some thematic possibilities could be contradictory. Since a character consists of different radicals, each of them carries meaning of its own. So for *ao*, we may deconstruct it as a combination of the top and the bottom parts. Regarding the top, the outside looks like a square or a building without the solid base. What's inside? The character 'rice.'"

"Rice?"

"Yes, there're a lot of old sayings about the importance of rice in ancient China, so symbolically, anything important to you, money, capital, job, it simply dependent on whatever perspective you're taking at this moment."

"Capital," she echoed in spite of herself. For the Red Dust Lane project, the worst case scenario was that after making the initial investment, she would not be able to push ahead with the demolition and construction because of the resistance on the part of the residents in the neighborhood.

"I see. The possibility of your capital being stuck somewhere, for instance." He added after a theatrical pause, "Now let's take a look at the bottom part. It's the character 'big.' As a rule, the horizontal stroke is not completely connected with the 'square,' so the rice inside could easily slip out. Consequently a big risk."

"Go on," she said. It seemed to be increasing relevant to the potential project. But a fortune teller would be capable of making his statement ambiguous, yet suggestive enough for a client to follow along the line. "What's your overall interpretation."

"It is not we who make the interpretation, Madam," Chen said, "but the interpretation makes us—"

"So it's just like *tuishou* practice in Bond Park, isn't it?" she said, musing over the repartee. "Not that we push *tuishou*, but that kung fu practice pushes us."

"Exactly, Madam. But I would like to say something first. Your handwriting is extraordinary, 'like a dragon soaring and like a phoenix dancing,' like in an old saying."

"You don't have to say that," she said, dismissing it as a bogus compliment.

"Now the square on the top of the character looks like a cage weighing heavily overhead. Your being no ordinary woman makes the square a big one, possibly concerning a lot of people."

"Wow! What else can you read in the character?"

"For what time period do you want to know?"

"The near future."

"There's something weird," he said, having restudied the character for one or two minutes. "For the bottom part, because of its position, actually resembles that in the character ji--the foundation for a house."

It was astonishing, yet not too surprising. Everybody was thinking and talking about buying or selling houses in today's China.

"And look at the way the character is written. For some people, the top and bottom parts do not appear to be sealed tight, so what's in between—the rice--may leak through. But yours is different. So closely connected, that surely will make a difference."

"What are you talking about, Sir!" She stared at him in spite of herself.

"About all that I can read in the character, Madam. A possible turn for you in the near future, I'll say."

"Can you be a bit more specific?"

"Some important people might come to your side. Believe it or not, what eventually helps you, however, arises from your own heart. The Way of the Heaven is mysterious. It's imperative to remain pure in one's heart and do good things."

It sounded like a warning, but it was perhaps conventional for a fortune teller to end up by giving "to-do-good-things" advice, which would never go wrong.

"You are no ordinary fortune teller, Sir."

"In Buddhist scriptures, identity too comes as an illusion, like a bubble, like a lightening. Today you take me as a fortune teller, and I am the very one for you. But I've told you all I can possibly read in the character, I think. So please pay me for my reading if it is not too far off the mark. It's getting late. I'm afraid I have to go back now."

She produced five hundred yuan out of her purse.

"Thank you for your extraordinary reading."

"No, I don't take any more than what's due to me." He picked up two one-hundred yuan bill. "Thank you, Madam. Bye."

He stood up, carrying in one hand the chair with the scroll sign draped over, and the stool in the other. Then he turned, smiling over his shoulder before disappearing into the lane.

So he lived in the lane, she reflected. It's easy for him to come out for the practice. She, too, was about to turn when she came to a sudden halt, as if his parting smile had stricken in her a forgotten cord, yet suddenly familiar again.

"Oh excuse me, Sir. Do you have a business card?" she said in a hurry, stepping up, lifting the bangs from her forehead. "Some friends of mine may also like to use your service."

"Sure. That will be fantastic." He produced a card, which showed only his name, along with a telephone number printed underneath. No address, except for the name of the lane.

Master Chen Cao

54171006

Red Dust Lane

The name clicked. Was it him? The one she had met first in the park in the early seventies, and then in the small eatery in the late eighties. The man she had since cherished in the memories, which turned confusing, however, even then and there...

But how could Chen have come to that?

Holding the business card, she looked up to see no trace of him left in front of the lane.

After all, it could just be a coincidence, another man with the same name, she speculated.

Not too far away, an old rag picker could be seen passing by, looking around, and dropping scraps of the minute into a bamboo basket on his back, his face as weather-beaten as a Qing terra-cotta figurine on a postcard.

She turned around to the group sitting out there, in which several more people had joined. She moved toward the white-haired man talking in the center, who was possibly in his mid-seventies, grasping a purple sand teapot in his bony hand.

"Excuse me, Sir," she said, addressing him respectfully. "I've just talked to the fortune teller—"

"So you're the one coming in a Mercedes," a middle-aged man cut in, having probably caught sight of her stepping out of the car earlier. "What did he tell you?"

"Don't worry about it," the old man said to her with a toothless grin. "Whatever he has told you, you don't have to take it too seriously. A learned professor he might have been, he is not exactly a qualified fortune teller—in the profession for only about two or three years."

"A learned professor—" she echoed, her heart missing another beat.

"Not just a professor, but a poet too. A real celebrity in his day!"

That's him. No question about it anymore. Glancing at the business card in her hand, she recalled another one from his hand that night many years ago, with his university position under his name. The effort to juxtapose the two cards in her mind overwhelmed her, with all these years written and crossed out in between.

She tilted her head up at a flash of the dying sunlight on a blue jay's wings. All these years wasted like a dream...

"Chen," she repeated to herself, almost inaudibly.

Fragments of memories arose in confused alarms. Those days in the park, she had hardly noticed him—just one of the young people playing tai chi in the tiny square. Nor could she really recollect how she had quit studying English. But if his presence there had somehow contributed to her decision, she should have been grateful to him for it—a crucial link connected with another, and then still another, in a long chain. And years later, another link in her eatery that night, when he gave her a business card, and looked back over his shoulder, smiling and encouraging. In the days afterward, she had read about him, being so proud of his success. She did not try to contact him, however. He cared for her, she knew, but not as a struggling proprietor of a shabby eatery. So she made up her mind to do something in her way. Coincidentally, her business began picking up at the time. She became so busy, hearing nothing about him any longer. Thanks to China's reform, people had more choices for themselves. Some went abroad to study or work, and for a scholar like him, it was not something unimaginable. He should have been successful wherever he went, she believed.

"Have you heard of him before?" the old man asked.

"Yes, years ago. I read one of his books. How has he come to this?"

"So you're one of his fans?"

"Has he had lots of fans?" She asked her question without responding to the one raised by the old man.

"Well, fifteen or twenty years ago, but not a sing one left today—except you."

"Oh please tell me what has happened to him."

"Tell her the story, Old Root," a bespectacled man urged with tangible expectancy in his voice, pouring water into the cup for the old man, and pulling over a bamboo chair over for her. "You have thought so highly of him."

"Confucius says: *he who seeks virtue reaps virtues, and he who seeks righteousness reaps righteousness*. Alas, neither virtue nor righteousness is worth a penny in today's society. As for what has happened to him, Yingchang is the one to tell." Old Root turned to another man sitting in the group, who was probably in his mid-fifties, with beady eyes and a high forehead accentuated by a balding hairline. "You're at the evening talk of Red Dust Lane, a time-honored convention here. So Yingchang will tell you the most authentic story."

"And you're coming to the very story teller, the real story, Madam," the man named Yingchang responded with a chuckle. "I've known Chen for forty years, growing up together in this lane, playing lots of games, like chess, crickets, and tai chi--"

"Tai chi?"

"Yes, that was at Bund Park, during the Cultural Revolution, but for only a very short period. He switched into English studies there. Because of it, he got into college in the late seventies—with the highest English score in the college entrance examination. And it did not take long for him to make a name for himself in the academic world. While still in his thirties, he was made a professor. A star born out of Red Dust Lane, as people all said. Toward the end of the eighties, he was given a prestigious fellowship to go to the United States, but he chose to stay here—for a series of academic books. Strange indeed, but that's what I heard.

"Then came the summer of 1989, when students started protesting in Beijing. In Shanghai, he did not have to do anything. An impossible bookworm, he believed in so-called principles. So he met with western correspondents and issued a strong statement, speaking out in front of the camera: 'If the government fired on the students, it could not but be a fascist regime, and I would give up the Party membership.' The troops fired out a couple of days later. Some government official approached him, suggesting that he was drunk the day he made the statement. Can you guess what a response from him? He declared that he had never touched a drop in the morning. And for what he did and said that summer, he refused to make any "self-criticism." On the contrary, he kept his word by turning in the Party membership card. That left no choice for the Party government."

That threw light on his sudden and total disappearance from the official media, she thought with a sinking heart. That summer, she had a hectic time opening a second restaurant in Jin'an District, where she saw students taking to the streets, causing terrible traffic congestion. She placed bottles of water outside the restaurant, marking "free for the students," but Ouyang stopped her. Some people got into serious trouble afterward, she knew. But she had never thought of Chen in connection.

"So he was fired as one involved in the counter-revolutionary activities against the Party government that summer," Yingchang resumed, taking a long sip at his tea. "Not a too harsh punishment, considering the circumstances, he could have been sentenced for years. People tried to help, giving him money in secret, which he declined. He shut himself up in his attic room and translated literary theories all day long. For years, however, no publishing houses were able to publish his work."

"But how could he have supported himself without any income?" she asked.

"It took tremendous efforts for the neighborhood committee to secure the city minimum allowance for him. To be fair, it's a real credit to Comrade Jun, the head of the committee then," Old Root commented, nodding at a gray-haired man in the back. "But that's not much, I mean the minimum allowance."

"Things then improved a little," Yingchang went on. "No longer under close surveillance, he managed to have one of his translations published under a penname. But China had been changing too fast. Disillusioned after that disastrous summer, people lost interests in modern or postmodern theories. Look to the money, that's all about it. His work became too irrelevant.

"But he refused to mend his way. He started a small bookstore named Red Dust, stocking mostly the academic books that did not sell, and shutting his door to the bestsellers. Now let me give you a real example. A 'beauty writer' contacted him, trying to organize a book release party at his bookstore. It's an attempt to capitalize his name as a serious scholar, no question about it, but to be realistic, very few remembered his name by that time. So it might have been a fantastic opportunity for his business too. He said no, however, on the ground that she wrote with her body rather than with her brain—"

"How did you know about all that, Yingchang?"

"Because the 'beauty writer' happens to be a distant cousin of mine, and it's me that I introduced her to him. What a face loss for me! And it's just a matter of time, as you may imagine, for the money-losing bookstore to go bankrupt."

"The story is no story," the bespectacled man cut in again, spitting on the gray ground. "The water flowing, the flowers falling, it is a changed world."

Not too much of a story to the people here. But not so with her. However unbelievable to others, what had happened to him seemed to have intertwined, so intricately, with what had happened to her. She felt overwhelmed.

"I did not know—" She did not know how to go on. But what if she had known?

"You're concerned about him," Yingchang said, looking her in the eye.

"I read his books. He's so brilliant. "

"But what? People nowadays judge a man by the money he makes, which he has none. You're the first one to have asked about him for years."

"Was he always so bookish—even when you practiced tai chi with him in the park?"

"He's a different duck, as early as those days at Bund Park. And here is another anecdote about him. Something I alone can tell you. We went to the park to practice tai chi, you know, but can you guess why he suddenly switched to English studies? Because of a girl sitting on a green bench there with an English book on her lap, on whom he had an impossible crush. Instead of approaching her directly, he tried to impress her by holding an English book too, reading loudly on another bench close by. But then he was hooked by the book, studying like crazy. Impressed, she made him numerous encouraging signals, which were all wasted, like water off a duck's back. She was so pissed off, she did not come to the park anymore."

That last part was not true. She had never given him any signals. For that matter, she could not remember anyone reading English loudly in the park.

"When the fish is caught, the net is forgotten," Old Root commented again.

"Did he tell you all these details, Yingchang?"

"The lovesickness was written all over his face—with all the unmistakable details in an open book." Yingchang said, pinching the jaw between his two fingers. "She's not exactly a knockout. Looking back, I'm still wondering what he really saw in her."

Whatever Chen had seen in her—during the days in the park, it was obvious that Yingchang did not recognize her.

But Chen did not recognize her, either—not this afternoon.

Had she changed that much? For him, she could have been an idea—an embodiment of the youthful idealism in Bund Park, holding a book—now incongruous with a prosperous-looking, middle-aged woman, carrying a LV purse.

"Like in an old saying, the woman is trouble water. She made him, you may say, because of her, he started studying English in the park, which led to his academic success, but eventually, to the disaster in 1989."

In an instant of illumination, what Chen had said to her that night came back to her, "I think I have now made up my mind—after tonight's—"

Could he have made up his mind—because of her—to stay on for the book project in China?

If so, was it because she meant such a lot to him? She could have been flattering herself too much. But there was no ruling out that possibility. That night, having given her the business card, he must have expected her to call. But she chose not to do so, for reasons hardly understandable to herself.

On the other hand, if she had contacted him, particularly during that tragic summer, would she have been able to calm him down? Perhaps he might not have reacted so emotionally—

"Something wrong, Madam? You suddenly look so pale," Yingchang said with undisguised curiosity in his voice, "like you have just seen a ghost."

"So that's how he has come to fortune telling?" she said, not answering the question, and then added in spite of herself. "Does it make enough for him?"

"Not much. He has really to scrap along," Old Root said with a wan smile. "But with things so unpredictable in the world of red dust, fortune telling is coming into fashion again."

For a fleeting moment, she was tempted to tell her story to the group she had just met in front of the lane. A real story about the unpredictable in the world of red dust. About those dew-decked mornings in the park, and the night in the eatery, the lambent light wrapping the two of them up like in a white cocoon, the stars whispering out the window...

But she checked herself. Telling such a story for what?

Perhaps as the raw material for gossips and speculations here in front of the lane. Telling the story now did not make things change or happen, incapable of bringing her back, or him, to those long ago days when they still had the opportunity to make different choices for themselves—

The cell phone started screeching, like a cricket under the green park bench in the memory. The screen showed Ouyang's name. The third time during the day. Possibly for something urgent. She chose not to press the talk button, however, in the company of the lane residents.

And she was having a second thought about the project. The people appeared to be truly enjoying themselves, talking and yarning in front of the lane, with the evening spreading out against the sky, with light clouds rolling in changing shapes, careless of what might come the next day.

He, too, had just been here, sitting out on the street corner with occasional customers passing by the lane. If he was relocated to a new apartment complex in a faraway, hard-to-reach suburb, she failed to imagine the continuation of his practice.

"Will the practice of fortune telling get him into trouble?" She asked again.

"It is done in the names of the *Book of Changes*," Old Rood said. "Nowadays you may see it as part of the classics rediscovery, about which there is even a popular TV series. No problem for him to make a modest living out of it. For all you know, there could be a lot of profound learning in fortune telling."

"You might make a good profit," Yingchang said with a meaningful grin, "if you chose to invest in him. Actually, one of his customers suggested that he set up an office with a neon sign at the entrance of the lane, but it may not be easy to get a license for that."

"And it has to be a large office," another one in the audience cut in, "not that small attic of his."

"The real question is," Old Root said, "whether he wants to do so."

She made no immediate response, not sure whether Chen himself really believed in fortune telling. In this new century, however, people were willing to pay for a "divine oracle." So that might actually work out: *Red Dust Fortune*. She could help to secure the license for him. That would not be a problem. She knew a number of people in the city government. With the business set up properly, he did not have to struggle on in dire poverty.

He was special to her, she knew, not just because of their encounter in Bund Park, or of the subsequent one in the restaurant. Of a sudden, she was full of admiration for the man he was, uncompromising for all the changes in the materialistic age, and adhering to his conviction at what an expense to himself.

"Mencius says, 'A true gentleman he is, not confounded by money or rank, not subdued by poverty or hardship, not bent by power or might,'" Old Root said, as if somehow echoing her secret thought.

So it was up to her to help this time, her thoughts in a swirl. She could secure a large office for him too. Perhaps a luxurious suite in one of those upper-scale buildings somewhere, where he would be able to attract Big Buck customers. In Hong Kong, a successful fortune teller could also be a millionaire. She might even provide an office for him in her own office building. There was a suite recently available on the first floor, perfect for the purpose, she recalled. Like the long-vanished green benches in the park, their offices would be close. After all these years, they had so much to tell each other...

It might not be too late to start again. For a moment, all possibilities came crowding up in her mind, but she then reminded herself that she was no longer that young girl in the park.

The blue jay flashed its wing once more in the dying light.

She produced her phone and texted the driver to pick her up—at the same spot near the back entrance of the lane, before she rose to take leave of the people in front of the lane, bowing to Yingchang, and then to Old Root.

"Thank you for telling me the story about him, Yingchang, and thank you, Uncle Old Root, for speaking so highly of him."

Then, should she go ahead with the business plan, as suggested by Ouyang, to raze Red Dust Lane to ground?

She decided that is was not a moment for her to worry too much about that decision.

Turning around the corner of Fujian Road, she looked back over her shoulder to the dust-covered lane in the glowing dusk. Red Dust Lane.

She found her eyes moist with a siren coming from the river.

Made in the USA
Las Vegas, NV
24 October 2021